# THE EAST IS BLACK

# THE EAST IS BLACK

*Len Bracken*

# A NOVEL

THE EAST IS BLACK

iUniverse books may be ordered through booksellers or by contacting:

iUniverse
1663 Liberty Drive
Bloomington, IN 47403
www.iuniverse.com
1-800-Authors (1-800-288-4677)

ISBN: 978-1-4917-5530-3 (sc)
ISBN: 978-1-4917-5531-0 (e)

Print information available on the last page.

iUniverse rev. date: 08/21/2015

To Ines

"Come in ladies and gentlemen! Come in! What you've never seen before you won't see here either, but it's an inopportune menagerie nonetheless."

Walter Serner

# CHAPTER 1

The Steinheil riflescope compressed the distance across the lake in a trajectory aimed at a young woman as she stripped for a swim under a diluted morning sun. His enhanced masculine sight targeted her flesh—slender ankles rising into shapely calves and thighs; thick brunette pubes growing on a smooth pelvis; high breasts swaying as she stretched. After his years of ideological training, the state security agent with an eye on the scope thought of her as a fascist body he longed to socialize. He would, he was sure, show her how communal manifestations of life confirmed social life in a socialist republic.

Her delicate neck and face belied her crude, as he saw it, submission to religion. She's from the same mold as the women who voted for Hitler, the agent thought as he watched her wade into the green lake sixty kilometers outside of Berlin. Ghosts from the past clouded his mind with vapors of confusion. The former Olympic athlete turned totemic-keeper-of-order indulged in vague fantasies of the German Democratic Republic capital as Athens on the River Spree, of the object before him as a classical nymph in a pond. He was a man of the world, or so he thought, in the general sense that he had studied Plato at the sports institute and in the limited sense that he made his part of the world his possession—a notion at odds with a true mann von welt[1], who might instead simply examine her personality in the context of ideologies and sexual capacity.

For Adina, who was now 20, this cool body of water enveloped her being and penetrated her orifices, giving a deep feeling of belonging. As soon as her nipples touched the surface, she lifted her feet from the silt bottom and brought her legs and hips up to the surface. She floated for a moment, providing the agent with an unmoving target of upturned breasts. Oblivious to him focusing on first one and then the other areola, she gazed into the clouds as the liquid cooled her head and penetrated her ears. Above all she loved smelling the lake's grassy scent when it was close to her sensitive nose.

At moments like this, she didn't so much go out into the world as let it enter into her inner experience where her instincts spoke to it in intimate ways. An only child who grew up in the sleepy town, Adina was naively solipsistic, which allowed her to unselfconsciously float face-up in the nude. Having spent much time with just her mother, or alone, or in nature or with mute animals, she was the logical, though seemingly contradictory, product of her surroundings.

With the exception of its meager tributaries that ushered in twentieth century industrial waste, the lake was frozen in time, as if seasonal cycles still meant more than five-year plans—a place where male aggressivity and female passivity were still the fundamental sexual psychologies stressed by her parents, who did their best to shelter her from socialism by recreating a nineteenth century idyll sixty kilometers southeast of Berlin.

---

[1]    A man of the world

Her father, Günter, abandoned himself to labor; and her mother, Beata, struggled for a religious life while weaning Adina on homegrown swine and cabbage, Christian parables and folk tales about the viciousness of bears. Yet her mother increasingly spoke to Adina about the importance of sex and the perpetuation of life as if Church doctrine meant less and less to her. She taught Adina about animal beauty, for instance the two of them watching male bees grab and mount females when they emerged from reeds and flying away together in airborne love feasts, and in many other ways her parents encouraged her to cherish the reproductive cycles of nature. At moments like this, when her husband was too busy working in the garden for romance, Beata loved thinking of her offspring and of herself—through her daughter—as a pair of freshwater prawns. The older woman imagined the two of them stroking through the water about to be taken by large males.

Adina's white arms glowed in the smooth gray-green water as she whipped them in graceful breaststrokes and kicked like a frog, each kick making her protuberant white ass wobble and flex beautifully. Head bobbing up and down with each long stroke, acid rain water inundated her mouth from time to time. And as she gushed it out, invariably some would seep down her throat and become part of her.

The same was true of the city for this country girl. Bit by bit, surreptitiously, Berlin was in her belly—dust from the windswept plazas and useless gray zones, the smell of coal-burning tile ovens and the sensation of being on the edge of her world near the infamous wall. I must be more careful, she thought as she inevitably sipped a few gulps of lake water much the same way the irresistible flood of socialist propaganda swirling around her ecosystem seeped into her mind more so now that she worked in the city.

But the propaganda had always been there, even in her small town. Her father once returned home from work on a construction brigade to find his young daughter playing with a doll that held a red flag glued to a lollipop stick:

"Not in my house. What is this red flag doing in my house?"

Adina, at six, looked up at her father with a frightened pout and hugged her cat.

"Easy, dear," his wife cautioned, "she doesn't understand what it means. She just does what they tell her to do in school. Besides, flags seem glamorous to her now. It's something we all grow out of."

Beata covered up the doll and the child's color pencil drawings emblazoned with red flags.

"I don't like it," the husband countered.

"I don't like it either. God will answer our prayers and one day Adina will forget her red flags."

Günter grumbled something about being cursed by God as he walked to the garden. He was happy only when working, so it was a welcome surprise to his wife that they'd managed to conceive Adina. Beata liked to say that passion was not in his vocabulary, except a passion for hard work. When asked if he was happy, he would respond by enumerating his possessions, which included his wife and child. Beata indulged her husband's notion of property, but in truth she ruled the roost and belonged to the Catholic Church. She rose at daybreak to go to mass every morning, where she routinely met with others on political issues. It was because of Beata that Richard—the agent from the Ministry for State Security—surveyed this country cottage. She led her local church in prayers aimed at the wall: "Let us pray to God that change will come," she cried to the parishioners, ignoring the fact that change was constant.

Richard could afford to amuse himself for a moment and focus his attention on the lovely daughter's swimming technique because the mother's priest was an informant. From the priest he learned everything he needed to know about Beata at church, such as the fact that she had been "married," as they say, in bed five times in one night at a carnival, and that Adina was no longer a virgin, having been deflowered by a windsurfer after a regional regatta when she was 18. He sighed at the poverty of Adina's spiritual horizon, what he confusedly thought of as petit-bourgeois hedonism that led her to act so blindly—a brief tumble in the bushes at twilight with a young man who was also a virgin.

Adina reached the opposite side of the lake, no longer in mother's view, coming ashore on the banks of a slender finger of water. Richard still enjoyed a surplus of vision with his scope, training the cross hairs on her while remaining unseen less than fifty meters across the water. She stretched her languid body on the bank, forming a mold of her protuberant buns in the mud. Her eyes closed and she remembered the way some bitches rub their vulvas on the ground when there are no males around for them to woo. A fissure opened in the clouds and the filtered sun fell on her, embracing her warmly from a great distance.

This was her communism, if the term applied to her, a sexual communism in which her entire body was in communion with the forest and its chaotic luxury of love organs. She thought of the way randy ducks attack each other, but Richard could think of nothing other than to commune with her as man and woman, and then make her the communal property of his water polo team. She opened her eyes and vague, seemingly manlike movements and passing shadows appeared underwater, feeding her intuition, which was nurtured by primitive country living to identify with animals and their spasms of birth, sex and death. A sweeping organic sensation flowed through her as she nestled in the mud, oblivious to the designs Richard had for her.

Despite his disdain for this decadent woman, this church-going, windsurfer-fucking fräulein[2], he was nonetheless impressed by her and longed for the hedonistic sensation of what his ideology held to be the object of his desire. Perhaps it was because he was out of his environment—the joyless downtown core of East Berlin. Or was it, he wondered, simply the associations of water and youthful beauty? Whatever the reason, he wanted her swollen petit-bourgeois vagina and partially mud-covered breasts.

She slowly bent her body backwards, and in his mind's eye he imagined his tongue sliding in and out of her slit. Even more than usual—as he set aside his rifle and took off his shirt—he felt the blind confidence men like him have that they're on the right side of history. He would turn her, in time, of that he was sure; and when he was finished with her, she would be an emblematic socialist woman he could put in a swimsuit so as to let her curves speak for the state. He walked into the water, headed directly toward her.

Adina reveled in her deep trust in the world, in the clean air and plants, the water, birds and fish around her on this late summer morning. She was head cosmetologist at a Berlin beauty shop who extolled the virtues of mud for one's skin. Now she packed more of it on her own long legs and flat stomach, being careful not to cover her breasts; she knew from experience she would kiss her pink nipples. For now she could forget the wall and all the voids created by the fences, lights

---

[2]     Young woman.

and watchtowers that she associated with the city, as well as the hall-of-mirrors sensation she often had amid the cerebral chaos created by close living.

She rinsed off her fingers and raised her right breast to her mouth. He slipped underwater and whipped his body like a seal while propelling himself forward with his arms and legs as if flying underwater. Her rectum expanded, opening like a sea anemone, as a wavelet rushed under her legs and hips. The wet sensations from the mud dripping down her vulva induced a deep sigh. He suddenly surfaced in the shallows.

For the veteran water polo player, ten strokes underwater were trivial compared with other complex stratagems he sometimes used to find himself in a similar situation. He wasn't even breathing hard. The opposite was true of Adina—her tit fell from her mouth the instant Richard's broad shoulders eclipsed her sun. Her eyes widened and the corner of her mouth affected an enigmatic smile. He stared down on her with a domineering smile.

"What," she asked, "are you doing here?"

"You're like a flower here in the sun—of course I want to be close to you and enjoy your scent."

As he drew near, his eyes were subterranean rivers, and as he knelt next to her, with the sun at his back, the glassy orbs picked up glints of light from the wavelets. He grazed the black stubble on his cheek against hers as if they were old friends. She panted at the sensation of Richard's flaccid yet prodigious cock that swayed across her and pressed into her while instantly hardening. Her transfixion by his eyes snapped and she noticed he was still wearing the domineering smile that created deep creases in his face. Adina rolled over and crawled away on her hands and knees.

"You have to be nice, or else stay away," she said.

Richard maintained an insulting silence as he moved toward her mud-covered ass and deftly clutched her ankles. Without much effort, he pulled her into the shallows. She squirmed slightly, as if half-accepting that she was being carried away. He playfully washed the mud from her supple body with caresses and allowed her to slither free for an instant.

"I just want to make a little commerce with your body," he said.

"How much will you pay?"

"What did you say?"

She shook her head. "I was only joking."

Suddenly, his ruthless grip terrorized her and she realized that only a communist would joke that, only it wasn't a joke, rather a warning. She screamed weakly as he took her further in. Her feeble kicks—softened by water—were parried by a deep scratch to her shaven calves. He kept his toenails sharp for water polo to scratch his opponents.

The sensation and sight of blood flowing from her leg shocked her a bit and she gave in the way she had seen, on so many occasions, queen bees give in when they emerged from the shoots and the yellow-striped males latched on to them— the way her mother had taught her. She wrapped her arms around his torso and buried her face in his dark chest hairs. As he tightened his grip, her breasts pressed against his stomach, her nipples rubbed against the ripples as they bobbed up and down in the wavelets.

His growing cock poked her in the belly, then the pulsing organ slid up—soft skin on soft skin—between her breasts as he pushed her down. To her it felt stupendous, like an arm against her chest, but she couldn't see it in the murky water, and when the base was between her breasts, the tip wrapped part way around her neck. Bending at the neck, clutching the tip near her ear, she tried to get a better look. All she saw was the massive girth of a small section and blood rushed to her loins.

She convulsed slightly, feeling herself opening and being slightly inundated with water, her legs trembling and her grip loosening on the snake as it slithered down her torso and he pulled her with big hands by her youthful, sleek ass.

"You can have everything for free," she said as she wrapped her arms around his stout neck and positioned herself, moving willfully, so the tip of his dick lodged in her opening. "I'll be the one who pays."

He took her into slightly deeper water, applied force, and for an instant backed out a bit and water filled the voids. He winced in pain at the pleasure foregone. Her wet flesh throbbed for him, and she took a sideways glance at the deep wrinkles around his eyes. He is much older than his athletic body indicates, she thought, almost as old as my father, but here he is between my legs with his stupendous organ. Her vulva dilated and oozed into the water like a fish laying eggs. There is no way, she thought, this communist member will enter without brute force. She felt his biceps tighten on the left side of her waist. His powerful hand clasped her right hip. Bubbles and white froth seethed around them. His hips pumped the rod into her yielding yet unaccustomed flesh while his arm held her in place.

She gasped then cried like a wounded animal from the tearing sensation between her smooth, kicking legs, spurring him on to smoothly back in and out a bit, and in and in still more. Once deep inside her, he turned, and like the bees fucking while flying, he began to swim away from shore, keeping her head up, pushing into her as they went. It was within his might to take pleasure from her, and, as he saw it, it was his right—granted by her playing the bashful belle. She regretted the role and now feared the brute with his machinelike, giant eggbeaters for legs and one arm holding her masterfully while the other stroked near the surface. His rod displaced any water there was in the depths of her vagina.

Yet he was more than a well-practiced machine, more unrestrained and unforgiving—there was something wild about what he was doing. She had committed the high crime of femininity and he would punish her for it by mangling her most sensitive spot, by boring her out to new proportions, by drilling her with his horrendous auger while effortlessly bobbing her up and down around the lake. He wore a look of shrewd confidence on his face that hinted he could drown her with nearly every stroke, kick and pump. She bit into his neck.

He unflinchingly continued rotating his legs at the knee and squeezing her waist—a little bite on the neck was nothing in his exhilarated state. "You know, it only takes a little bit of water to drown," he said.

Fear flashed over her passions, which instantly won back the battle for a conscious response. She heard herself wail in the most wanton way, possibly in earshot of her mother.

"Be quiet," he said. "Listen to the water."

She heard him and the water flowing into his voice and sloshing back and forth in her mind. Trusting the intelligence of her instincts, she displayed it through murmured expressions of desire in her voice and with her trembling legs.

"That's good, my little oyster." He guided her back to the shallows, where he could stand.

Compared with his wife, she thought, he probably thinks of me as fresh meat—all he has to do is detach me from my shell and he can eat me alive. In truth, her vibrant, resilient, willing flesh was almost too much for the old man. Her desire excited him most—what he saw as an innocent, instinctive desire born of youthful curiosity and a sumptuousness that was beyond her years. Her will to come satisfied the orders of her organs as her nerves were raging with sensitivity and other senses conspired to reinforce her genital sensations. He in turn did what his genital apparatus demanded and flooded her tender sluice with aging socialist sperm. She clawed his back with manicured nails, tracing stinging arcs that pulsated through his massive body along with more pleasurable orgasmic spasms. As the wavelets died down, he gulped some air and receded into the lake without a trace.

# CHAPTER 2

A middle-aged woman entered the shop; fresh air dissipated the nail polish fumes for an instant. Over the whir of hair dryers, the rap beat pulsed on radio waves: "'Heels tall, bikini small, she said she liked the ocean' . . . We just heard 'Goin' Back to Cali.' And now the US Armed Forces Radio News for October 6, 1989. Speaking on the anniversary of the birth of the German Democratic Republic, visiting First Secretary Gorbachev stated 'We are prepared for anything,' which is the Russian leader's clear acknowledgment of the protests and illegal crossings over the Hungarian border by East German citizens."

Adina knew enough English to understand. As she teased the old woman's hair, memories flooded her mind—receiving her Hungarian visa on the fourth of July and listening to the same radio station on the long drive in her little plastic dog, as she called her two-stroke Trabant car, contemplating escape while traversing Czechoslovakia. The old family friend hadn't been home. Adina stayed with his neighbors, whom she didn't really know. She felt scared and alone, but also nervously excited. Freedom was only a few kilometers away. Nobody—not even her mother—knew what she was doing. Drinking wine from a bottle, she followed another German Democratic Republic car through the night to the border. The car ahead of her was stopped by the Hungarian police. She turned back.

Walking the streets of Budapest, she had hoped to meet some other young women but a car pulled up with a Yugoslav inside.

"Shall we go?" he asked, opening his car door, flashing tickets.

"What is it?"

"A rock concert."

"I've never been to a rock concert. You know, the tickets in GDR are controlled by the Free Youth Organization and I don't have a single red friend."

"Don't worry," he said. "I'm not red."

At the concert, she drank more and more wine. The heavy yet somehow lighthearted rhythms of the drums and guitars were delicious for her ears and made her want it to keep going. On the way back to her car, he pulled over in the meadow. He was so rough that she didn't dare fight too much—she was afraid he'd hit her and ruin her skin. Holding her hands over her head, he tore off her panties and stabbed her with his prick.

He came instantly, groaning, "I didn't want to do it."

"It was my fault," she mumbled.

The old woman whose hair was in Adina's hands looked up. "What was your fault?"

"Oh," Adina uttered with a forced laugh, "nothing."

It was better if nobody knew, not even her mother. The customer sighed impatiently. Adina worked more quickly. She was the brigade leader and tried to set a good example, first by finishing the perm and by cleaning up. She was perturbed that the two other cosmetologists were standing by the window, smoking.

"Let's clean up so we can go," Adina said as she swept the floor.

One of the other workers motioned out the window with her cigarette. "Take a look—a wedding."

Adina joined them at the front of the shop. Although she rarely smoked, she extracted a cigarette from the pack on the sill of the big front window without asking. A gray, joyless day. Clouds hung low in the sky, effusing a constant drizzle. The cold humidity seeped through the window. Her coworker struck a wooden match. Adina shuddered as she inhaled. From their shop on Otto-Schmirgal-Strasse, the young women looked through the rain, across the road and tram tracks, to Tierpark, the old zoo built in the fifties on the grounds of a former palace. A wedding entourage laughed at the bears as they lumbered over the rocks or dove into the water after pieces of bread. One stood up on his hind legs and waved for more with his massive paw.

"I can't wait until I get married." The young woman put out the match used to light Adina's smoke with a puff of smoke from her own freshly lit cigarette.

"Me too." The second coworker patted her hair. "Think of the time she'll have tonight. What do you think, Adina?"

"He looks a bit thin to me. But what do I think? I told you what I think. We should clean up and go. I have a long train ride home."

Even from that distance, across the four-lane boulevard and over the zoo wall, the sight of the bear standing on the hillside gave her a faint, blood-swelling sensation, an organic sensation that reminded her of the man in the lake who had ravished her several weeks ago, then vanished underwater. She felt a tinge of the power and the danger in the memory. This feeling, however pleasurable, was clouded by the memory of the Yugoslav in Budapest. She looked away and then continued sweeping, lost in thought. Had she let herself be taken again? The tools of her trade absentmindedly fell into place. Finally, the others called goodbye and turned the lights on and off as they left.

She sighed heavily, always—as the manager—the last to leave. Out of the corner of her eye, she gazed at herself in the mirror, at her forlorn beauty as she took off her work jacket and put on her overcoat. Feeling slightly sorry for herself, she walked the length of the long, narrow room. The hollow sound of her shoes on the tiles echoed in the concrete ceiling. Adina glanced back at the shop and turned out the lights.

The rain fell on her as she locked up and finally turned away from work, opening her umbrella and bracing herself against the weather. The first steps on wet footpaths strewn with trash led to a path surrounded by apartment tracts made from concrete slabs sprayed with silicone cement above, and at ground level, a pharmacy, library, restaurant and government offices. From the restaurant window, a waitress with an enviously small waist waved to Adina.

Adina waved back and moved on—the waitress was more of a customer than a friend. What she needed now wasn't a customer or a coworker but a genuine friend. She continued walking, crossed two lanes of traffic and hesitated at the U-bahn[3] entrance, a block-like concrete structure half-buried, out of the rain, under the middle of the road. It was easier to take the train than to drive all the way home, but if she had driven she could linger in the city. Without my car, she

---

[3]     Underground railway.

thought, I have to hurry home after work without talking to anyone, no chance to go out for a drink or at least have another look at the bears.

With a quiet sigh she lowered her umbrella and began collapsing it, but decided against it. Street lights in twilight— she wrapped her hands around the umbrella and opened it again. A force, perhaps one as banal as boredom, carried her away from her train, up a set of rain-swept steps to the other side of the road where she waited before the other two lanes of traffic.

Liquid traffic lights shimmered on the wet pavement as cars came to a stop. Walking into the oncoming drizzle, she squeezed the umbrella grip with cold hands, gazing into the drops illuminated by the now-still headlights. If the bears have any sense, she thought as she crossed the street, they won't be out. But they were there, seemingly unaffected by the cold rain—big and strong looking. Adina stepped across the sidewalk and watched, huddling under her umbrella. She looked over the wall, contemplating the bears' captivity. She was lost in thought when a voice broke her trance.

"The symbol of Berlin."

Adina gasped, startled to see the man from the lake standing next to her. "I, I didn't think I'd see you again."

"Here I am. I often come to Tierpark, when I have the time, to look at the seals," he said, barking like a seal, "Arghhh, Arghhh."

His head was cocked back and well-defined neck muscles bulged out past the side of his head. With that mustache, he really did look a little like a seal. She had that organic feeling again, only this time the sensation was more giddy. She again giggled.

"I don't know why I'm laughing," she confessed as she lifted her umbrella up for him and ran her hand under his green nylon jacket, behind his back. "Can you imitate any other animals?"

He wrapped her neck in a half nelson and gently flexed his biceps. "This is what you call a bear hug."

She laughed again as he let her go.

"You laugh," he said, "because of the Berlin air. When it rains like this and the air is alkaline and full of oxygen, I feel as if I've had half a bottle of champagne. Speaking of which, would you have a drink with me?"

He asked the question in familiar East Berlinerisch[4]. She nodded so as to not draw attention to her country accent. They began walking and passed the wedding station adorned with wreaths. If marriage was crazy like love, he thought as he directed her to his light-gray Wartburg, a two-door roadster parked in the police zone in front of the zoo, I might try it again. But it isn't.

"My name's Richard," he said with a smile.

He opened the door for her. She smiled. The fact that he parked his car where he did, that he didn't ask her name, would make most GDR citizens wary. So would his mustache, his green nylon jacket and the white tee shirt that clung to his massive neck—clear signs he was from the Ministerium für Staatssicherheit, or Stasi, as the state security ministry was commonly known. Adina suspected as much but felt weak and wanted to be with him. When he started the car and turned up the heat, her legs felt warm way up high, around her tender inner thighs. He turned up the fan.

"Where are we going?"

---

4    A dialect of Berlin German.

"I just remembered something," he said. "A friend of mine asked me to look after his apartment while he was away. Do you mind if I stop there for a moment to water the plants? We can have a drink there."

Adina nodded and watched him swing a left onto Frankfurter Allee. She wouldn't go to a dance club with a stranger for fear he was dangerous, but she was blindly going to some apartment with this almost machinelike man. She wasn't thinking clearly and knew it. He calmly drove through the rain. The Lichtenberg Bahnhof[5] flashed by on her left. She glanced at her stainless steel watch—her train was leaving. She never had time to live. Now was the time. She was in his hands now.

He glanced over to her as he drove. "Have you ever heard of water polo?"

"Like a kind of water ball—I think so."

"The friend I'm helping is on my team. We'd do anything for each other."

So that's why he was at the lake, to train for his water ball, she thought. It made sense. Richard glanced at her sharp, innocently alert features while turning left, down a side street. Two blocks.

"Do you want to come up?" he asked as he pulled up to a rare old apartment building with intertwining jugendstil lines that had survived the war. "His place is really nice."

Adina followed, wiggling her ass uncontrollably as she walked. The metallic tic of the rapidly cooling motor. Someone shuffled down the street. A loud hiccup. The drunk crossed their path on the sidewalk, then turned back.

---

5     Train station.

"Will you have a look at my lingerie?" he said in heavily accented German.

He opened his nylon bag. The Stasi agent clenched his fist. The guy slunk off in fear, walking backwards. Stumbled.

"Polish swine." The towering athlete groaned through his teeth as he grabbed her hand. "Come on."

The Poles were to blame, according to the agent, for the present wave of troublemakers. Everything was going fine until their underground culture moved the communist center off the map in the seventies and eighties. See what they are now, Richard thought as he held open the door, a bunch of lingerie salesmen. Adina looked in the entrance at the marble floor, crystal chandelier and wrought iron elevator. At his behest, Adina moved ahead in the low light. She slipped on a stone chip on the first step and her foot turned on its side.

"Hey there," Richard said, a sure hand ready around her waist, helping her regain her balance.

She gasped and fell into his arms, biting her lip in pain. She inhaled sharply. In a smooth movement, he scooped her up and carried her up to the next landing. She sat with her legs falling back down the first few stairs.

"Are you okay?" He leaned over and massaged her slender ankle. "We'll get some ice on it and you'll feel better. Here, I'll carry you."

"No, let me rest for just a moment."

He nodded to her pouting face and stared into her brown eyes as he continued massaging her ankle. His gaze shifted with a sidelong, admiring glance at her long Prussian legs. Before she could protest, he scooped her up and carried her upstairs.

"This used to be a nice place," he said. "The bourgeoisie really knew how to live, as much as I hate to admit it. Hard to get an honest repairman these days. Most of the other tenants have moved out." He took more stairs in silence. "Before long, the building will be condemned."

A shaggy youth skipped down from the third floor and glanced at Adina. "Pollution must really be getting out of hand, man. You should take her for a cure in Rostock."

The Stasi agent flashed a brutal smile, a nonchalant gesture that he mastered along with his rage. His white teeth glimmered in the streetlight that shone through the stained-glass window. He lowered Adina to the stairwell. As he raised himself to his full height, he turned back his jacket collar with his free hand to reveal the insignia of his water polo club. The kid stepped down the stairs, clutching the rail, looking back. The athlete's smile became more genuine, more full of mirth, finally breaking into a hearty laugh. He could twist the scrawny kid's spine into knots, which was Richard's idea of a really good joke.

"Sorry," the kid said as he scrambled away. "I never should've mentioned the contamination."

Richard laughed at the notion that the kid thought Adina was contaminated, when he was the one whose mind was obviously suffering from ideological contamination. Powerful arms picked her up and the couple continued up the stairs, Adina lolling doll-like with her calves draped over his forearms. He grunted up the last few steps to the fourth floor landing and eased her legs down. A deep sigh issued from her mouth as he held her with one hand while he fiddled with the keys in the locks with the other, then swung open the oak door.

"Wonderful," Adina said in awe of the apartment, half-forgetting her ankle and the incident on the stairs as she pushed away and tried to walk.

He followed her across the threshold into a completely remodeled flat that contrasted sharply with the run-down building. Track lighting illuminated the textured paint on the walls and the paintings that had been confiscated from the studios of nonconformist artists who subscribed to decadent art theories. Adina was particularly struck by several female nudes lolling in the grass and eating grapes as a jet raced over the sky and a tank was positioned in the woods.

Another wall was lined with freshly polished trophies. And between the front windows looking on the street was a large aquarium containing brightly colored fish. They swam happily after the worms Richard dropped in the tank. The kitchen, she noticed, had every convenience—many Adina had only seen in magazines, like a microwave and dishwasher. While he was busy feeding the fish, she took in the tools scattered on the dining room table: a suitcase encased two-way radio, a time-delay clock for use with detonators, gas tank pills in foil packets that make car engines break down and other instruments she couldn't identify, such as a pair of infrared voice links—metal-boxed lamps on little tripods—used for talking over the wall.

"What are you doing?"

Adina turned. "I was just looking."

"Don't worry about that stuff. Come over here."

She sat down on the couch and massaged her ankle. He popped the champagne cork.

Richard extended the glass with his brutal hand. "Can I get some ice for your ankle?"

"You really have ice?"

"Yes."

"Well, no thank you, I'll be fine."

"Come now, trust me, you must reduce the swelling."

"No, I told you I don't want ice. I don't want to feel cold, and besides, it's not so bad."

Richard shrugged and then switched on the radio tuned to a classical station. She continued massaging her ankle as they listened to the Berlin Philharmonic play Bach. The technical virtuosity of the composer's fugues was not lost on him. He actually knew the orchestra and had listened to the song in person, but he loved the word orchestra for other reasons, for its use as a euphemism for espionage organizations working against the Reich, such as Moscow's red orchestra. The champagne bubbles tickled their noses, yet his mind was never far from work.

Adina felt the rhythm caress her soul; it gave her body the urge to dance. She guzzled the drink, not noticing that Richard merely raised his glass to his lips without actually sipping—knowing that he could be called to duty at any time. He was so strong looking, she thought as she inhaled the scent of male sweat in this communal bachelor pad, where she was sure he and members of his water polo club brought their mistresses. Her nostrils flared wider as she sniffed the residual aroma of the Stasi agents eating meat after killing.

Adina sighed, emitting a slightly plaintive tone with her breath. "I think this champagne is wonderful, don't you?"

"Yes. Just what I needed tonight," he lied.

She crossed her legs toward him, briefly exposing her thighs. Then, as if she were bored or nervous, she bent forward and propped her elbow on her knee, bobbing her foot to the music.

"If you want to be touched," he said, "just tell me."

She buried her forehead into his shoulder. He lowered his arm around her back and stared ahead blankly for an instant.

Then, without disturbing her head, he stroked her hair with the opposite hand.

"Be honest with me, Adina. Tell me what you really want to do."

He sensed Adina's repressed excitement, noticing her bobbing ankle and the scratch on her calf—by now almost completely healed. He had given it to her at the lake with his toenail. It reminded him of the bite on his neck.

"Why did you bite me at the lake?"

"Why?" She rolled her eyes. "Why did you rape me?"

"That wasn't rape."

"Maybe I bit you because I was hungry for you."

"Are you hungry for this now?"

He unzipped his trousers. Because of her youth, her relative inexperience, Richard wanted her slowly this time, in a way that would have her come back sooner for more. Adina, as soon as she caught sight of his cock, wanted his rough hands on her breasts right away.

She dropped her glass on the carpet and reached for his hands. His cruel grin mocked her desire as he grabbed her by the hair, telling her, "No teeth," while lowering her and fully pulling out his cock.

She had an artistic sucking technique, developed since she first procured what she thought of as pimple cream during adolescence. She reached for his belt buckle. His scent made her nostrils quiver, sending shivers down her spine. She marveled at his size, more like a bull or a horse, she thought. Richard watched her dress ride up her hips, over her swollen buttocks. Her taut round spheres stretched the lace fabric of her panties into transparency. This thin veil provoked Richard more than any naked ass.

The provocation was in the potential for unveiling, and in the fact that her panties were from the west. Although his pleasure was, in principle, a just reward for security service to the socialist economy, he took her decadent display of bourgeois culture as a personal affront. She has no social conscience, he thought, she half-believes in the humiliating Christian morality that depends on God's will. She held him with one hand and as he hardened, felt his hot, smooth flesh against her cheek. It wouldn't have mattered to Richard to know he had drawn a fallacious conclusion because as Stasi, he considered himself categorically exempt from the contradiction of social and personal interests. He watched her do what she wished with his dick. If she wants to experience the degradation of the individual, he thought, I'll oblige her.

Through this act of bare negation, this humiliation, he, the masculine subject, transformed his object—now she conformed to the image he had of a proper Stasi slut. Never mind that she loved physical affection like any other mammal and wore western panties for the simple reason that levels of production lagged in the east.

He rudely picked her up by the ass as he stood up, pulling off her panties as he walked her down the hall. Something snapped in Adina. Out of fear for his strength, she sensed the need to put a limit on Richard's freedom of activity with her body—not to be taken so easily. She stroked his hair as they entered a room that, unlike the rest of the apartment, hadn't been remodeled.

Richard's thick neck and heavy eyes resembled those of the Prussian generals in the paintings on the wall. Rain pattered on the window. A streetlight threw striped shadows on the bed. The iron bed creaked from her fall on the polystyrene mattress. Hysterical laughter wafted up from the street. He removed his belt and placed it on the head rail. His eyes met hers as she watched him strip. She was fascinated by his brawny shoulders, creased muscles and black chest hairs flecked with gray.

He pulled his belt out of the loops. "What are you waiting for?"

"Schmusen.[6]"

The Stasi agent was not a partisan of the cult of intimate feelings. He scarcely noticed his object's consciousness and by no means would he conform to her wish for affectionate caresses.

"Roll over."

"No, I want to kiss," Adina said.

Richard snapped the belt across her thighs and she felt the intense heat of pain.

"No, don't," Adina protested as she rolled over, onto her belly.

Luckily for Adina, her powerful libido was disseminated throughout her body and could attach to almost anything, even the crack of a belt. His violent efforts to punish her for wearing western panties gave her great pleasure; her buttocks swelled and reddened as they clenched and unclenched, her rectum expanded and contracted to her cries. He founded his consciousness on official discourse, which made him appear socially sane, but even this ideological monster was not immune to the organic sights and scents before him. From the look on his feverish face, Adina thought of him as a wild animal, of her as his prey.

"Strip," he commanded.

Half out of fear, she wiggled out of the dress colored in browns and reds that hinted at her powerful drive toward

---

[6]  To cuddle.

sensuousness. From the joyous hues of autumn leaves she sensed deep down that death, like sex, was beautiful. Her nipples hardened from the cool air and exposure to the eyes of this dangerous beast. Adina pushed her big, gelatinous tits together.

"Suck these."

The agent stood over her with a belt in his hand. And in the context of their positions in the room, her command was more a plea. She reminded him of his daughter and he felt a tinge of contrition at the welts he made on her ass, a pang of remorse that led him to indulge her request, if only for a moment.

Her nipples were extremely sensitive; they exploded with sensations from the touch of his tongue. With his mustache stippling her white and pink skin with red spots, he pulled her breasts together. The sides of his tongue rubbed each nipple and his whiskers tickled. He stuck them in his mouth and sucked them between his lips. The tip of his tongue flicked one, then the other nipple, teasing the knot of nerves fanning out from her areolas. Her great, pushed-up breasts were firmer than ever, begging for gentle squeezes.

Lightning flashed in the room, followed by a roll of thunder. Adina felt vulnerable and hot. A moody Beethoven piano concerto played on the radio in the other room. Richard looked up at her in the dim light of the street lamp. He moved down her body gently licking his way to her long, slender legs. From her calf, still scarred and covered with light fuzz, he nibbled and sucked his way to her hairless inner thighs, toward her inflamed pelvis. Her fur-trimmed slit was wet; he flicked his tongue over her hot clit. She twitched, then pushed his head away.

"I'm afraid," she said, hastening to add, "I sense your energy."

"Don't worry. It's been so long since I've been with a woman that I'll probably only last a minute," he lied.

He drew a line with his tongue around her sex, a line lost in the shadows of her thighs only to re-emerge up her belly and across her breasts. Adina drew in her breath in anticipation of his kiss, the delicate taste that failed to arrive. Instead, he pressed his skull next to hers and stabbed her gash with his member. She buckled at the waist under his pressure and groaned deeply. He reached under her and massaged the contusions that had issued from his belt a moment ago, greedily groping her ass. He sucked her ears, pausing to whisper that this was how she would learn about love.

She writhed under the pressure of his body. Squirming with pleasure, yes, but also squirming with fear as she strained to breathe.

"Not so deep," she murmured.

Her words were lost on the man who had a compulsive need to demonstrate his athletic prowess. This wasn't a delicate genital embrace so much as conquest whereby his virility and her submission were the issues at stake. She sensed his power in her burning tissues, his incredible strength, which made her feel light-headed. But she wished he would be gentler so she could feel the sensations surging through her body in a more sensitive way. But he wasn't.

He surged in and in, with skill, but without restraint. She delivered herself to this monster and the thrills he created everywhere, although she tried to grip the base of his cock with her hand. She felt his surges from the nerves in her thin red labia to the scorching recesses of her vagina. He pressed too hard for her hand to stop him and even with it between them, he still went too deep. Thoughts of resistance vanished. With a tilt of her pelvis, she rubbed her clit on his striated stomach muscles. Shuddering in orgasm against him, letting out a gentle cry, a tear rolled down her cheek.

Shrugging to his teammates and fellow Stasi who suddenly appeared in the doorway, Richard let out a strange animal groan that was echoed by the others barking like seals. Adina looked up, startled, but when Richard wrapped his elbows around the backs of her knees—the seal noises continuing—she was, once again, overwhelmed by sensations to flow into the situation, to answer their call and Richard's controlled deep groan with a few whimpering moans. Richard is thrusting more gently now, she said to herself, just as I liked it. He suddenly stopped as if he didn't want her to like it too much and moved some of his massive body off her delicate body, petted her...her hair, her face and breasts while looking into her eyes. With Adina looking back into his eyes, the slackening tip of cock slipped out with a thin gush of semen that bled from her labia into her first line of fur.

He watched his cock slip down, deep between her legs, between her dripping cunt and her lightly wrinkled asshole. She squeezed him with her wet thighs at this bridge of sighs, rubbing her creamy slit up and down on his shaft. Something moved near the door. Adina sat up, clutching the sheets to cover her large, pointed breasts.

"You're beautiful, so don't be shy," Richard said soothingly.

Adina clenched a fistful of sheet. "I don't like it."

"You're only a babe. You don't know what you like or don't like," Hans said with a domineering smile.

Richard kissed her on the forehead and pulled at the sheets.

"No, I won't." Arrogant laughter flooded her ears before she could finish her phrase. "I won't let them see."

"What you don't understand, honey," Gerrit said in his grating voice as he moved forward and the men ritualistically exchanged bone-crushing handshakes, "is that we're Richard's teammates, his brothers. What's his is ours, and vice versa. I'm surprised he didn't tell you that when he brought you here."

"He told me he had to water the flowers or something of a friend, that's all," Adina said in disbelief.

"And so he has." Hans mimed with his hands watering women's breasts, as if he had a pair of his own. "Now we want to water the flowers."

"But I'm not his property," Adina said in protest as Hans and Gerrit neared the bed.

"You're property of the state," Gerrit argued with irrefutable logic, "and we are the state."

She looked over at Richard, who merely nodded in agreement. Adina's last fleeting vision—before she was hoisted onto the athletes' shoulders, before her horizon began an irreversible downward spiral—was the gold insignia on a green nylon jacket of a seal balancing a striped ball on his nose, a boa twisted around his neck, etched in fine detail, right down to the fur and snake skin. In low relief below the image was the word Stasi.

Adina felt faint. She bobbed up and down while being carried through two thresholds into a low-lit room. A black marble hot tub was situated in the center under a skylight. She heard the gurgling of water jets. They lowered her into the liquid and she realized how her body ached, how her every muscle had strained under the weight of orgasm, how good she felt to be submerged in bubbles. Richard was there too, reclining on the edge of the tub like the dominant seal in the herd—his cock lewdly fell over the side and received a massage from the hot water jets. Adina closed her eyes and sank deeper into the tub, her breasts floating on the surface, her nipples begging for attention despite her apprehensions.

Startled by a wavelet, she opened her eyes. Hans and Gerrit were with her in the Aquadrome, as they called it. They moved toward her. They're younger than Richard, she thought, and just as fit, only not as big. Gerrit took her foot in hand and massaged it with his thumb, moving to her ankle having no idea of her slip on the stairs, of the soothing effect this had on Adina. His intent was to trigger reflexes and excite her genitals.

Hans took a seat behind her on the edge of the tub, straddling her back with his muscular thighs. He massaged her neck using his open palm. Adina felt his hardness on her upper back. And below, she was melting, not from the water, but from inside out. Hans ran his fingers through her thick brunette hair; he grabbed a fistful of hair on both sides of her head and massaged her scalp with gentle movements that indirectly stimulated her elsewhere. She felt a warm flush travel from her belly to her bowels.

Richard rolled over a bit and flipped a switch that triggered a ring of water jets on the hot tub bench. Adina spread her legs and moaned as the jets hit her bottom. She shifted, then lowered her fingers to her clit. Hans and Gerrit exchanged weak smiles at this display. It shocked them, but only mildly.

"Seems like she's enjoying herself too much," Gerrit said. "What do you think?"

Adina looked up at the blond-haired, blue-eyed man who held her head in his hands—Hans nodded. Gerrit, who had massaged her feet, turned her over by her legs, so her clit lined up with the jets. The rigid prick belonging to Hans, which was surrounded by blond pubes that had rubbed her neck from behind only an instant ago, was now under her nose. Hans guided her head to it. With her hands on his hairy thighs, Adina took his member into her mouth and bobbed up and down. Saliva soon dripped from her juicy lips down his balls.

Gerrit slipped between her legs from behind. Her back arched, and she presented her round cheeks and private parts to him. She was almost ready, but he couldn't wait, not a moment. She wasn't ready for the quick violent thrusts—violence directed at a woman replicating the relations of dominance in everyday life. They were men only when they were violent, so they were almost always violent, or at least aggressive. Hans held her head down and Adina gagged on his penis, ostensibly a sign of her female passivity. He chuckled at the sounds that came from her throat.

With their one-sided vision of sex as power, the men were half-blind to the aggressiveness of Adina's lips, blind to the power of giving pleasure. As she feasted on them fore and aft, the men obviously knew she was giving and receiving pleasure, but it was beyond their powers to fully understand how she was obtaining power over them from her gift-giving acts of love. Her eyes glazed over, her vision clouded. She fused with these two men. But she also attained a new degree of organic autonomy through them by rapidly expanding her capacities and by partially negating the men—giving in not so much to them as to her sovereign instinct for pleasure.

The bubbles from the jets tickled her inner thighs like champagne or whiskers. She bucked her rump back into Gerrit. And with every pump, her sexuality grew stronger. She sensed she was submerged in a faceless yet unified intracorporeal experience—the plastically consummated woman, sensing desire from the other and his double, and possible triple, with or without them. The sensation of her nipples dipping in the water as she bobbed and bucked obviated everything else.

She leaned back and disengaged her mouth, rubbing her breasts. "Suck these."

"Yeah," Gerrit sneered in his metallic voice. "Don't just sit there. Suck her tits."

Richard smiled the bemused smile of a voyeur made aware of his voyeurism. It was obvious Gerrit found this subversion of Richard's pleasure pleasurable. Hans, on the other hand, liked to watch people watch. Ultimately, though, Adina was the one who got what she wanted. Richard rolled off the edge into the tub with a splash—he submerged for an instant and emerged between Adina's breasts, in the space between the water surface and the edge of the tub and her lovely torso. With one giant hand, he held one nipple with his thumb and index finger and the other nipple with his ring finger and pinky. Her breasts came together nicely as he pulled on them.

"Kiss them," she begged.

Richard felt as if he were indulging his daughter, who was a little older than Adina, but he did so without reluctance. Her nipples squished inside his mouth—her double suns blotted out his entire horizon, ushering in a vague reminiscence of his mother's mammary glands. Like all infants and savages, Richard had a terrible fear of incest. In a way, the gift of his mistress was like giving away his daughter to members of his tribe—the gift assuaged his guilt. Adina's beautiful, young body was obscured by her formidable cleavage, but Richard sensed his teammates' ministrations that caused her such writhing pleasure.

Despite an infantile desire to kill his friends, to regain exclusive possession of his symbolic mother-daughter-lover, Richard continuously sucked her tits beyond the point when his lips became sore. Just as Adina derived a perversely childish pleasure from the paternal crack of his belt across her buns, Richard was aroused when she nursed him. It triggered an obscure memory and desire to reunite with it.

Richard maintained his lip-lock on Adina's nipples while he pulled Gerrit's cock out of her cunt, knowing Gerrit would deflower her rectum. Like many of his countrymen, Richard had elevated his mother to a spiritual ideal of love and respect. The conquest of her bowels by Gerrit, taking place simultaneously with Richard's re-entry into her vagina, was a double-movement: on the one hand it rendered Adina a virgin, thereby distancing her in Richard's psyche from his mother and approaching that of his daughter; on the other hand, this debasement made him lose all respect for Adina.

Richard glanced up when he heard Adina's animal wail that was muffled by Hans' cock. He could see the organ bulging against her throat tissue as he felt her insides contract and release incontestably at the onslaught of two cocks in her lower tubes. Never had she been so inundated by the outside world, never had she submitted to such a radical restructuring of her anatomy. She imploded and exploded at the same time as though her tissues dissolved and the limits of her body expanded with each thrust.

Hans sensed the electricity in Adina's mouth as she moaned, but he was more thrilled by the open-lip image, which was his compensation for a voyeur's lost playfulness. He spurted in her mouth. The halting groan from Hans and his bitter white aphrodisiac on her lips made Adina think her soul flowed from her tongue. The seed of life and another little death carried the contagion of passion back to the others as if they lost the beginning or end of their bodies. After Hans, Gerrit came first, then Richard. One right after the other. One, two, three. Adina liked it, the surging male energy and the warmth of their seed. Richard kept sucking tit, Gerrit pulled away, out of her backside, and slid into the swirls of water. The phone rang.

Gerrit climbed out and answered: "Un huh, I understand."

"Who was it?" Richard asked.

"Headquarters. They want us to go to the Linden and look for troublemakers."

The men dressed, loaded their tear gas pistols and headed for the door.

"What should I do?" Adina asked.

Richard turned just before leaving: "You can do what you want."

# CHAPTER 3

Weeks later, on a day when the beauty parlor was closed for a public holiday, Adina emerged from a book shop on Unter den Linden[7], the formerly notorious boulevard known for its pedestrian mall in the center of the street that was now in a bleak mood of forced joy as parade marchers filed by, longing for the liquor waiting for them at the end of the route. With her freshly coiffed hair and a new dress under her overcoat, Adina felt beautiful, as beautiful, in fact, as the models in the west. But she would never know because she could never compete with them and it wasn't worth it anymore to model for reds, which is how she thought of her talent manager.

He had spotted her when she was organizing cosmetic seminars at enjoyment centers in Berlin. It wasn't long before she met, through him, people from the clothing factory. Modeling for reds didn't pay, and her manager was always pestering her to fuck him. For that he would pay. Better to

---

[7]    Under the Linden Trees.

live a quiet life, her mother told her after she'd heard about it. Adina had second thoughts.

It was a lead-gray day toward the end of October. Playing taratara, a military band stepped past her in uniforms reminiscent of the Reich. The Day of Public Health.

Adina was a striking sight as she strolled along the majestic, broad street that had once been so lively. She would have stood out even in prewar Berlin. There were so many beauties then, it was true, she thought, but how many of them had studied nutritional science and massage? Adina pictured those outlandish women with provocative, pantherish strides and sensual elegance; women who were likely to be nude under their overcoats.

Adina remembered how it felt to go braless on the runway and this reminiscence made her smile to herself. She glowed amid grim-faced parade-goers who embodied the colorless sky in their skin. Dwarfed by the open expanse of the street, the few spectators blended with it, their presence scarcely felt. No immense multitudes formed in the end of East Berlin despite government exhortations. The worker state was like Rome during the Middle Ages, nearly empty, on the verge of being swept into the dustbin of history by disintegration to its east and smothered with commodities from the west.

She followed alongside the parade in hope of sensing that carnival spirit that her mother loved so much, thinking about how much more of it there was on the other side of the wall. How lively and wonderful it must be. Her aunt and cousins who lived in the west were so carefree in comparison to Easties. Adina looked in the austere display window of a woman's clothing shop. She was conscious, in a detached way, of the frustration she lived with every day, all the time—depending on parcels from her western relatives to clothe herself; although she would, from time to time, make her own clothes.

Adina, reaching up to feel the leaves, reminded herself to wear those clothes more and to be herself. She harbored deep resentment for the fact that her relatives could visit the east and she couldn't go west, but she told herself, as her mother had told her, that this just made her stronger, more disciplined.

Walking again, Adina shot a glance at the Goddess of Victory at the apex of twelve columns standing in proportions like the Parthenon in Athens, which she had seen in her history book. The Brandenburg Gate to the city was now a dead end. Adina saw herself in the goddess sealed off by the wall but also rising above it—her new Grecian topknot was like a crown of hair, and, in a way, Adina felt like she had won a victory.

She had released her repressed, feminine drives in the Aquadrome. She found the experience both fascinating and repellent. These paradoxical sensations were, to her, so unfamiliar and uncanny that somehow in splashing over the abyss into infinite pleasure, her former identity began to disintegrate. Was this, she wondered, what it meant to be herself?

If so, she didn't really like herself, but the terrorizing pleasure she felt at the hands of the Stasis had distanced her from her mother and their ex-urban idyll. She was becoming more Berlinized, spending nights with Richard at the communal apartment where he made sure she liked herself by paying her inordinate amounts of attention. A new world opened up to her, but it didn't open far enough—she still sensed the need to go west. What a lackluster parade, Adina thought as she took in the muted colors. The parade moved on ahead. Good riddance. From what her mother told her of the old folk wisdom, there were once no spectators at carnivals, everyone got in the act and almost nothing was taboo. Now, in a tower on the wall, a guard focused his binoculars on the parade and surveyed the Unter den Linden, ready to douse the first spark of life.

Adina was still overwhelmed from instant to instant, step to step, by unarticulated sensations that were now almost always aroused. But they now seemed to depend more on a sense of danger. She recalled that during a recent trip home, walking in the woods, she felt bored like she had never felt bored before. It dawned on her that she had lost the sense of peril in being alone with nature. The city was now her forest; Richard and his dangerous friends, wild animals.

She picked up her pace and felt, as she often did, spied-upon. Instinctively, she turned up the steps to the Operncafé[8], formerly a princess' palace, now a people's restaurant. With the brass door handle in hand, she paused and looked in the bay window. Not too crowded. She strolled in, past the café and its tables set with unadorned Dresden china. She turned over a bread plate—Arzberg. Better, she thought, than any of the mass-produced porcelain they have in the west. Adina headed toward the wine tavern. The high ceiling was lined with ornate plaster molding that framed the tiles on the walls. Threadbare Persian carpets covered parquet floors.

The waiter, eyeing her entrance, approached before she could sit down.

"What would you like, miss?"

"Champagne," she responded, trying not to let his use of *fräulein* bother her by remembering her mother saying she was now a frau[9].

Adina pulled out her smokes from her purse and opened a book she had taken from the communal apartment library, *Sex*

---

[8]    The Opera Café.
[9]    A lady or adult female.

*Anomalies and Perversions* by Magnus Hirschfeld, the Einstein of sex and founder of the defunct Institute for Sexual Science in Berlin. A Turk suddenly appeared, thrusting a butane flame under her cigarette. Adina puffed, nodded thanks.

"May I join you," he asked in passable German.

"I'm trying to study," she said.

He glanced down at her notes in the margin of the book, then focused on her cigarettes.

"I see you smoke West. It's always amused me that the east would call a product that."

"Me too." She smiled weakly. "If you don't mind."

Adina turned back to her book, covering her face with it, perturbed at the thought that a lowly Turkish guest worker in the west would imagine himself a prince in the east. His ego was obviously out of control, she thought, if I give him an opening he'll probably try to sell me some cigarettes he smuggled from the west.

"Not at all, I don't mind at all," he said, looking at the title. "Where did you get that book? Did some homosexual give it to you?"

Adina waved him away with the hand that held her cigarette. Funny that he would say that, she thought, recalling how Richard said they had the book on hand as part of their research as to why homosexuals still existed in the socialist state. She took a drag to banish the unhealthy odor he left in his wake, which reminded her of a smelly Russian general she was required to friendship-kiss in her last year of school, when she was just eighteen years old. The champagne arrived.

As she took a sip, Adina scanned the bar. What does he want with me? The Turk was still there, at the bar, staring at her with bloodshot eyes, smiling with broken teeth. The greasy skin, she thought, he can't think he'll fuck me. With a foreigner? Ha. Never.

The idea sickened her. As much as she subconsciously aspired to become a cosmopolitan Berolina[10], for her this was more of an image than cultivating the requisite feelings of universal conciliation. She was hardly willing to share her land, much less her table or body with a migrant laborer, an undignified outsider. Adina was trapped in the east and, like everyone, trapped in the limits of her body. But more than anything, she was trapped in the prejudices of her people.

I don't like it, Adina thought, drinking up her champagne. She glared at him. Without waiting for the check, she fished through her purse and left five marks on the table.

The Turk had ruined her research, which was really a reawakening of the erotic bliss she knew from her infant explorations taken further and further. She had resexualized her thinking so there were moments when every gesture was an expression of Eros. She remembered the rape at the hands of the Yugoslav, and suddenly the Turk reminded her of the Poles who came to her village to sell their wares: one knocked on the door while another climbed through the window to steal what had been earned by hard work. She heard her father's hate-filled voice in her head, his warnings that the Poles would rape her and her mother.

The Turk watched her leave in a huff, his palms open pleadingly as if to ask, what gives? In her flustered state, she could never empathize with him, which would have been difficult enough under tranquil conditions. At the very moment, she was beginning to feel like a stranger in her own land—certainly in her village but also in East Berlin.

---

[10]     The female figure symbolizing Berlin.

She simply couldn't commiserate with a stranger. And her solipsism blinded her to hypocrisy. Had she been more human, she could have just as easily banished the Turk with her natural charm.

He followed her at a distance into the street. She saw him over her shoulder and stepped up her pace. They walked against the current of parade marchers who flowed down the street. Most onlookers were oblivious to the beautiful Berolina and the romantic Turk, but not Richard and his teammates, who were dispersed in the crowd. They signaled to each other with small mirrors and drew near. Exchanging a few glances, they immediately understood that she was leading a stalker into their trap.

With their green nylon jackets, white tee shirts, mustaches and the insignia of the water polo club, these four colossal men were walking totems whose presence was designed to impose social order. Yet neither Adina nor the Turk saw them emerge from the crowd. Two Stasi grabbed the startled Turk and sliced open his gut. The knives made no noise. All that was heard was the weak last gasp of a Muslim calling for Allah and the words of the other pair of Stasi who had grabbed Adina, words that fell between the poles of compliment and insult.

"That's what you get for being out alone."

"You gorgeous slut."

They all looked at the bloodstained corpse on the sidewalk.

"Who died?" one Stasi asked.

"Don't know," another responded. "Anyone's all right with me."

"Ha, you're killing me," a third said, breaking into laughter while the fourth Stasi radioed the police to pick up the corpse.

Eyes shot back and forth between the men and Adina and she blushed all over, feeling that sensation again, this time as a

wave of bashfulness. Her cleavage flushed red; they watched it
heave. One Stasi held open her coat by the lapel, showing her
nipple in high relief. Adina was no longer afraid of Richard
and his friends, of expanding the geometric configurations
of her sexual life. Although she was only eighteen, or perhaps
because she was only eighteen, these mature men found it hard
to match her sensuality.

Whereas the men conceived of sex as raw violence, she
had allowed eroticism to embrace her entire personality as
both the object and energy of her life. This transformation
placed her beyond men even when they were inside her—
while maintaining considerable autonomy, she used them to
consummate herself, to become more fully conscious of her
ego in the world.

There were eight members of Richard's water polo club.
When they were all together in one room discussing their polo
practice outings in the country, which was their best alibi to be
with their mistresses, Adina couldn't help but recall her fantasy
of having five men at once in her parents' lake. She longed for
spring, late spring when the water is warm. Although she felt
no jealousy for their wives, Adina did resent the presence of the
other mistresses on the outings—that was when she wanted all
the men, all to herself. Here, at least, were four. They ushered
her down the street.

She was the most beautiful and desirable of the Stasi water
polo club's mistresses, which made for awkward situations.
It was, after all, Richard who had said, "Do what you want."
Little did he know that she would translate his statement as,
"I'm ready for anything." Adina was quick to exploit the desire
Richard's teammates had for her and the jealousy this desire
might provoke with her rearticulation of Gorbachev's phrase,
"We are prepared for anything."

In the fairly recent past, Adina had resented the lurid looks men threw her way. She had equated their desire with hers, a mere wanting or longing. She was beginning to sense the desire of the other for her as something special. She saw past their violence, which was merely a mask of their desire for her desire. She sensed that giving her beautiful body was also giving her soul. She liked to think that in the eyes of the men this was somehow spiritual. As they sacrificed their hard-ons in her altar, she was becoming a goddess—the Goddess of Victory, in her mind. She brought about in these Stasi water polo players a desire for female desire, which, she sensed, deep down was also what they feared most.

Within moments they neared Alexanderplatz, the Alex. Heart of the east. The S-bahn[11] train hissed to a stop. Broken panes on the ironwork station. Graffiti gang wars on the hard edge, geometric structure at the base of the television tower: CITY FIGHTERS, REDSKINS (socialist skin heads), the A inside a circle transformed to an N with the stroke of a paint can, SIEG HEIL[12]. Groups of indolent youths and old women selling vegetables in the passageway to the square. As they passed the world time clock, facing the New York and Havana meridian, Adina again slipped into wanderlust. What's New York like with all those buildings and people, she wondered, or even the happy Cubans and their salsa music. Disagreeable smells wafted out of the subterranean public urinal, bringing her back to thoughts of hygiene on this Day of Health. The Stasis led her by the arm across the massive square past a conspicuous polizei[13] paddy wagon.

---

[11]   The rapid transit railway system covering the city and suburbs.
[12]   Hail victory.
[13]   Police.

They neared State Hotel—the closest thing to a skyscraper in East Berlin, a soviet version of a Bauhaus rabbit hutch. The group walked in as if they owned the place. To the visiting political dignitaries, businessmen and upper-level bureaucrats in the musty, modernist lobby, nothing seemed extraordinary about four apparently healthy men and a pretty young woman entering the hotel. The front desk clerk looked up from reading August von Cieszkowski and instantly knew better.

He pushed aside the book and adjusted his Brecht glasses, then nervously combed his slightly spiky blond hair with his hand, unable to conceal his discomfort. I'll just go on strike and give away the room, he thought. After all, this is the state approaching. Why should they rent a room from themselves?

"Good afternoon." He nodded to Adina. "Miss, gentlemen. What can I do for you?"

Richard leaned over the counter and flashed a genuinely confident smile. He thumbed the snake-and-seal insignia and its terrorizing five-letter caption on his lapel.

"We need a room."

"Of course."

The clerk turned to the key rack and selected a penthouse. He turned back and Adina stood before him, her breasts resting on the counter as she strained to understand the book title: *Prolegomena zur Historiosophie*[14]. She silently undid her hair pins and her locks cascaded down her neck like a pilsner overflowing a glass. She looked through the clerk's Brecht glasses—thick black rims, round lenses—at his blue eyes. He stared back at her blankly.

"Number 1545." The clerk gave Richard the key. "A penthouse suite."

---

[14]    Prolegomena to Historiosophy.

"Fine," he said.

The building, he knew, was true to its name and mirrored the vertical ordering of reality, east or west, wherever there was a state. Adina paused for an instant, admiring the clerk's Aryan features—he ran his hand through his spiky blond hair again. She thought he was cute and guessed he knew a lot about music and youth culture in the west. What he knew was the score, and he ignored Adina by returning her stare with an impassive gaze. Like many Poles, he was a linguist who spoke several languages with equal ease, which is how he got the job. Everyone mistook him for a Berliner, even the Stasi agents who ushered Adina into the elevator.

As the doors closed, one man fondled Richard's favorite tits. She closed her eyes and fell into his terrible arms. The others groped her and pinched her for the long moment up. The elevator shook to a stop. Like proper gentlemen now, they insisted that Adina get out first. She walked ahead, her long Prussian legs accentuated by high heels.

"This way, you idiots," Richard said. "You'd follow a naked woman right out the window."

Like most men, they followed the direction of their erections. She turned back, moved through them and found the room. Once inside, Adina turned and began stripping— first her dress, revealing her big, silk-encased breasts and matching panties perched atop her long white legs. Then the bra, leaning forward, unsnapping it from the back. Then the panties, one luscious leg—from curvy hips to pointed toes—at a time. A faceless Stasi threw her dress and coat on a chair; another pulled back the covers and sheets. Adina shivered with excitement and decided to stun them.

She counted out loud: "One, two, three, four . . . I want five."

"We can save that for another day," one of them said impatiently.

"The clerk . . ." Adina struggled to sound commanding. "Call the clerk and have him come up."

Instead of obeying her, they looked at each other, expressing an invisible code and attacked from every direction—she had hands on her everywhere and after that tongues in her holes and then everywhere she looked an erection invaded her body as if trying to stomp her to a pulp, making wine in an obscene Dionysian dance.

She strained her neck and contorted her hips to accommodate their members. She again counted out loud, squeezing each cock in turn as she did. One of the more playful Stasi picked up the phone.

"Hello, get me the front desk. The kid with the funny hair. Hey, this is room 1545. That's right, the four gentlemen and the young lady. Listen, the 'young lady' requests your presence, so get up here. If you have to, tell your boss a brother told you to take a break."

Another Stasi, one of the ones occupying Adina's lower body, conceded, "I can see why that Turk was after you." He had a low, hot voice, full of passion. "But you're strictly for domestic consumption. Got it?"

Adina nodded but was nodding anyway—she hungrily licked the knives that guarded her orifices from unlawful intrusions: their little sword swallower was willing to accept the demand of social allegiance so long as she was given their perilous protrusions for her pleasure. She tilted her chin upward, the lace of her tongue toyed with a cock, feeling guilty for not having sinned like this before. Someone's fingers kneaded the roundness of her ass, another cupped her thrusting breasts. He held them and felt her nipples rise to his touch. Another nudged her body with his, from underneath. Her hands searching, seeking and finding their hardness, fondling the round, rearing heads.

"Suck my tits."

Someone sucked her tits.

The clerk—who went by the name Jan—approached the room and reminded himself of his cultural superiority, of the pantheon of twentieth century Polish writers—Konwiciki, Gombrowicz, Lem . . . —and a few of the great modern philosophers often mistaken for Germans—Kant, Schopenhauer, Nietzsche . . . He would have to comply, like so many of his countrymen, with the imbecilic cruelty of Germans, but he would do so with honor and gallantry, or die. The door was unlocked. He entered. The tangle of bodies made it difficult for the clerk to make heads or tails of the situation.

"You made it," one of the Stasi said. "You should be glad, or else you'd wind up in the slaughterhouse."

Adina moaned, knowing that her fantasy would soon be reality. This transgression epitomized, in her mind, her new identity as an autonomous sexual being. The clerk hesitantly took off his right shoe, one trouser leg, shorts. All the while he was eyeing the one wonderful orifice to Adina's body that was less than fully manned.

"Let me see him," Adina moaned. He stepped to her side.

"You're beautiful," she said, looking past the Stasi agents with their hairy chests and big cocks at this hairless man she mistook for an Aryan.

She closed her eyes and rubbed her smooth ass, expanding and contracting it with a desire that displaced her desire to identify with her mother's provincial ways and provoked the Pole to thicken and harden. She felt energy and drive express themselves in her ass as she fucked herself on one Stasi cock, a fat one, frigged two more and sucked the fourth. Finally, the clerk knelt on one knee behind her and spat in her crack. He worked his saliva into her rectum with his thumb and spat again, this time in the palm of his hand, then rubbed his cock.

Trembling with excitement, he invaded and pressed into her body, expelling her mother with each purifying stroke that pulled him in deeper. The little rituals of hygiene that her mother taught her seemed absurd in the scintillating light of this cleansing. There's nothing dirty about me now, she thought.

Despite their proclaimed socialist morality, which would view sex as a healthy and beautiful side of life, these Stasi agents wanted, as Jan understood them, "to blacken the radiant and drag the sublime into dust," as Schiller said. He watched as the cock she was sucking spurted across her cheek, then in her mouth, leaking from her lips down her chin. This defilement exposed the lack of unity, the fragmentation of their egos, Jan thought. The clerk justified his participation as further disfiguring what was already disintegrating.

Like the corpse they so flippantly created from the Turkish worker, they were somewhere between beauty and filth, life and death—beyond reproach as they humped pretty Adina's hands and another came on her face.

The clerk carried on, working himself into her while rubbing her ass, satisfying what had been Adina's as-yet-unsatisfied desire. She was utterly confused as to the meaning of the cathartic energy that ran through her. These vein-bulging protrusions seemed what she needed to restore her edenic state of harmony and organic purity. The next one in her mouth suddenly exploded, then the other, the one in her pussy, pushing on the tissue between her tubes with his flexing cock, making her ass still tighter for the clerk.

While this was for her a cleansing, for the men it was like the dumping of military waste in her parents' lake—pollution rituals, red orgasms of anger that proliferated where male power weakened. She was impassive to this massive assault, hardly expressing her lust, which made them conscious of their wasted energy. And when it was almost over she rubbed it in by wringing more orgasms out of their slackening members—orgasms for her alone. The Stasi agents were nonexistent to her as men but as tools of satisfaction that were now in her power.

Only the clerk touched the core of her inner body where her spirit lurked. In these tight, dark depths, he turned her inside out, bringing the sickening smell of her slickness into the already pungent room. He transmuted her inner spirit into the soul of a German goddess, one who had no idea she was being fucked by a Pole.

# CHAPTER 4

Adina moved in with the Stasis and habitually walked around nude. She let them have their way whenever they wanted—when they weren't playing with their cameras to take photos through pinholes or shooting each other with video camera sunglasses…when they should have been monitoring protests that were taking place with increasing frequency since Honecker resigned as chairman of the State Council. Although the "black file" that forced his resignation had been prepared by other agents, the denizens of the communal apartment were aware that their boss had used the file showing Honecker's attempted Nazi collaboration to orchestrate the ouster at the politburo meeting in mid-October. Their arrogance half-blinded them to the pressure for reform emanating from the USSR, and they viewed the few protests they did monitor with contempt rather than alarm. Besides, they were preoccupied with socializing Adina.

As a joke for the others and to mock her, Gerrit had recorded her orgasms through a voice stress analyzer.

"According to the machine," he said, "her orgasms seem to be authentic."

"Yes, that one must've been from Richard," she said as a particularly lewd sensation came over her from the sound itself and from knowing that Hans was listening. "It sounded more potent than any orgasm I'd get from your little poison dart— you probably need one of those microdot viewers of yours just to see it."

Hans looked up from the cipher book he was studying. She glanced over to him as the orgasmic moans continued. The athlete stood, grabbed her and walked her around to the side of the sofa. He pulled it away from the wall a bit. She knew what was coming. He lined up her belly with the thick, rounded arm of the sofa and pushed her, face forward, so that her hips creased over it and her upper body rested along the seats. He undid his fly button and then grunted as he went in.

"Make yourself at home," she told him as he rutted into her upturned ass. "You can pound me as hard as you want."

She loved his smell when he got going—the animal scent and savage thrusts had her arms and chest pulsating along with her pussy, and her cries echoed those on the recording.

\*

On the second Thursday in November, she took the day off work and travelled home to her mother in the country. Her lovely ass shifted in the seat on the train and she felt semen drip from her box. The sensation made her wetter. If someone wants to take me into the bathroom and add his seed, I wouldn't mind, she thought. From now on though, I don't know how it can be with anyone who isn't an athlete. She glanced around the train cabin. No one was a match for them. Water ball players, she thought, they're the best.

Adina turned her coat over her lap and pulled up her skirt. Her panties were wet with semen and her own juices. Ich bin geil[15], she said to herself as her middle finger pressed into moist flesh. She rocked on her ass and then turned toward the window, squeezing the finger with her legs. As the countryside flashed by, she remembered how much she missed home. She was a little bitter because she had given herself, all of herself—her complete soul—to the Stasis. Only to be treated like a child. She was indeed like a child who wanted to please, a perverse child who granted them every favor.

She shuddered in orgasm at the thought of one of them standing on the couch in front of her with Hans behind. Her generosity with her womanly body was returned by making sure that all of her requests for a visa to the west were denied.

Richard protested the accusation of involvement in dashing her requests, and with his brutal politeness, he promised to suck her tits so she could forget about the west. Now she simply couldn't forget about him. She almost despised him now, as she journeyed home, and half-despised herself for her depraved acts of lust. But the thought of submitting to his force still excited her, deep down. She thought about it all the way home, about him and how much she wanted to see the west.

Her mother met Adina at the station and drove the family car, a burgundy, four-door Lada sedan. The tires raced over smooth roads. Ordered fields and farm hoses. Beata turned down the radio. "How is that man treating you?" Adina shot a glance back at her mother.

---

[15]     I'm horny.

"What?" Beata's expression grew incredulous. "I worry about you, you know that."

"Let's just put it this way. I'm in good hands."

"I'm sure of that," Beata said.

"What I mean is that nothing will happen to me when I'm with them. You know mother, there was a foreigner trying to bother me at the health parade. It didn't last long."

Beata drilled her daughter with a wary look as Adina cut a line with her finger across her throat. Beata turned the radio back up and they drove the rest of the way without talking. The car pulled into a shaded driveway in the late afternoon sun. Adina went inside and put down her bag; she walked through the living room taking in the familiar furnishings that triggered so many childhood memories. She could see the housekeeper through the window as she moved slowly around the garden. Adina stuck her head out the door and called hello to the now elderly woman. The housekeeper turned and smiled while bowing and waving with a fistful of radishes in hand. Adina smiled back radiantly and turned back inside. The sound of running water came from the kitchen.

Adina finally reached her room, a sanctuary that her parents kept as a shrine to their beloved only child. An old Irish setter, Peter, followed her into the room. Her shelves were lined with dolls and children's books; her grade school drawings covered the walls. She was reminded of her past researches into sex, which she had continued in new books and with the Stasis.

The sun set over the lake. Adina stripped and slipped into bed where the sheets were bathed in sensuous waves of pink and purple light. A voluptuous fever swept over her with the tawdry thoughts flashing through her pretty head—she glanced over to her little Peter sitting near the door and found in him the image of man in his barbarous and savage state as though there was a bit of Richard in him.

He looked up at Adina with eyes full of devotion. She was his goddess, he hadn't forgotten. His tongue quivered as he breathed quickly, sliding the pink tissue back and forth across sharp teeth. The things Peter and Adina shared during her childhood came back to her in flashes—walks in the woods, food from the table, secret games. She closed her eyes as a sense of enchantment with nature awakened inside her and ushered in that ineffable flush while passing her fingers across moist panties.

Beata walked down the hall reading a samizdat tract calling for the right to dissent, for freedom of thought and creativity. Unaware that Adina was in her room, Beata turned on the television. She knew the risks she ran keeping such literature in her house. The GDR retained Stalinist features longer than most other countries; it actually censored glasnost publications from the Soviet Union. Beata was a dissident, a member of the Church From Below (KvU). The church's credo, "Nothing grows from above to below," was refuted by stalactites and dominant males, but many people who knew better didn't quibble given such noble sentiments even if the leader in Leipzig had the regrettable name of Christian Führer. The church members used rabble-rousing tactics like storming the state-sanctioned church festivals with banners declaring GLASNOST IN CHURCH AND STATE while simultaneously providing cover for green, feminist and Third World activists.

The phone rang. Beata's husband, Günter, was calling from the west, where his construction brigade sometimes went as guest workers. "Hello darling."

"How are you?" she asked, rolling her eyes, looking up from her papers at the television.

"Fine. Fine. I thought only the reds knew nothing of work. Well, I had to show the capitalists what is the meaning of hard work, too."

"No one works as hard as you, Günter."

"You're right about that."

"Hold on, dear. There's some special news."

"What?"

"Just wait."

AKTUELLE KAMERA, SPECIAL REPORT flashed across the screen. A female newscaster spoke to the camera:

"The result of today's advisory meeting is a new travel regulation. According to government spokesman Schabowski, 'Individuals may now travel freely without proof of need due to exceptional or family circumstances.' He added that the regulation is effective immediately."

Beata gasped. "It can't be, can it? Could it be the wall has opened? They just said it on the news."

"I don't believe it," her husband said over the phone.

"It must be true." She shook her head. "The announcer said there was an official announcement. 'Individuals may now travel freely.' I'll get mother at once and come to you. Where can we meet?"

"I'll call your sister on this side and see you at Pottsdamer Platz."

"I hope we can find you."

"Look hard and you will find me."

Beata passed her daughter's room, where Adina writhed and her heart beat wildly as her fingers dug into her most fertile field, as if searching for a buried bone. She held her panties aside and burned with hot liquid as she spread her legs wider.

"Adina! When will you grow up?"

"Mother, I—"

"Come on, get dressed. We have to get Grandma—the wall is open."

"What did—" Adina started to speak, only to give herself up to her persistent fingers.

"I said, the wall has opened. Get dressed."

Beata slammed the door behind her, short-circuiting the erotic tension, the electricity that fused Adina's soul to her fingers. The wall has opened? Incredible, she thought. At last, the west. She sat up in bed in disbelief, then dashed to get dressed.

The Lada, with Adina behind the wheel, pulled up to a house where her grandmother, Maria, waited roadside. When Beata had phoned to give Maria the news, the elder woman was so excited and impatient that she refused to change clothes. She jumped in the back of the sedan wearing pajamas and a robe.

"I think your mother is lying," grandmother said to Adina.

"It's true," Beata insisted. "I heard it on television."

Adina laughed. "I think she's mad. Since when did Beata believe the news?"

"I know this government." Beata took a drink from a beer bottle. "We'll find out soon enough if it's real."

As occasional headlights passed the other way, Adina fiddled with the radio, trying to find some news. A bottle opened in the back seat, and Adina looked into the rearview mirror. Her grandmother was drinking and smiling at the same time.

"I hope we can find your father," Beata said. "By the way, do you want a beer?"

"Not while I'm driving." Adina pushed on the accelerator. "I can't wait to see if it's true and we can go to the other side."

"They can't keep us bottled up forever." Beata took another swig. "There might be some real opportunities for you over there. I always thought you should study acting."

"Maybe I will, mother. Maybe I will. At least I should be able to make some real money for my modeling."

Maria leaned forward. "Watch out for those modeling agency managers."

"You told her?"

"I was proud of you, Adina. These things are bound to happen and you behaved like a lady."

I was naïve, Adina thought. She stared straight ahead as the sedan devoured the road, thinking that the manager was actually quite handsome and she should've fucked him. Beata cracked another beer as Adina again fiddled with the radio. A cosmic blackness enveloped the country road; the headlights oscillated over the bumpy terrain, cutting a bleached line of sight on the dirt for an instant—then they dissipated in the night. Black telephone lines against the moonshine were occasionally obscured by silhouettes of trees.

Adina found a westie station: "I'm into you like a train . . . I'm into you like a train . . ." Hearing these lyrics and the hard-driving music, she wondered if she would feel comfortable and at home over there. After the song died down and ended, a news report stated that thousands were responding to the premature announcement by the East German propaganda minister of the new travel regulation by converging on checkpoints before the border guards had been instructed on how to handle it. People demanded entry into West Berlin and more were coming. The guards were outnumbered and letting people pass through.

Adina drummed her fingers on the steering wheel and then leaned into her safety belt around a bend. Her homeland already seemed somewhat alien, like a distant planet whose craters she rapidly traversed to get back to earth. It amazed her as she amazed herself—once her German rectitude was shattered by Richard and his friends she discovered this crazy passion, so seductively warm and inviting, that she simply couldn't deny it was part of her, even if it seemed so alien.

Mother will visit her sister, Adina thought . . . grandmother will see her other daughter. What will I do? I will find some way to have sex. Adina gestured for a beer; Beata handed her the one she was drinking and reached for another. Thoughts of sex, with whom she didn't know, flooded her brain. Adina drank some beer with one hand on the wheel. She drank more, squinted slightly, looking beyond her headlights into the unknown.

The national road Leninallee brought them into Lichtenbergstrasse. Storefronts and red and yellow cranes overhead. Adina put the bottle between her legs and increased speed. They went into a tunnel. As the lights lit up her face, Adina thought of the lyrics "I'm into you like a train." A street sign flashed by. She was grateful to Richard for having taught her the city so well, not just taking her places but showing her the major streets and how to find smaller cross streets on maps to get to just the right place without wasting time.

He knew the city so well, in fact, that he transformed it for her, making it no more intimidating than the woods near her family home. They came back above ground amid glass and steel buildings, and after a bit Adina turned left on Hans Beimlerstrasse, which opened up as it crossed Karl Marx Allee, only to narrow and cease to be a national road. The name changed from Gruner to Gertrauden and finally Leipziger as they drove into the Friedrichshain district. Shuttered shop windows, except for the older woman cooking sausages under the neon lights of an imbiss[16] stand—her arm quickly moving the meat off the fire with tongs.

Adina could tell that her mother was surprised by the confidence with which she handled the car, checking her mirrors and signaling—but not slowing down—as she changed lanes.

"I've always wanted to go to Wedding, mother. You know, the district in the former French sector." Adina switched to English: "Do you know what 'wedding' means in English?"

"No."

"It's the ceremony for marriage," she told her mother in German.

"Adina, you're not planning on marrying that water polo player, are you?"

"I don't know, mother. Now that the wall has opened, anything can happen."

Block after built-up city block. The traffic became more congested in the Mitte district. Adina slowed. Yellow and blue balloons floated across the sky tied together with white ribbon. She sipped her beer at a stoplight, smiling to the young people on the street wearing colorful scarves. There were always so many possibilities, she thought, and now there will be even more. She started again and drove on. Many people were walking on the sidewalk and even on the side of the street toward the wall. They slowed with the traffic and someone banged on the roof. Maria raised her bottle. Adina smiled nervously.

"Follow those cars," Beata said.

"I can see that, mother."

---

[16]  Snack.

The Lada took its place in the line at one of the six checkpoints that had opened. Adina felt more beyond herself from beer than usual. Maria was stretched out in the back seat. She gazed out the window at a car of young men also drinking beer and yelling that they couldn't get through soon enough. Maria toasted back to them, thinking they were nice-looking young men who would be good for her granddaughter. Beata noticed that one green bottle glowed and the kid with it pulled smoke from a tube. A firecracker went off and people in other cars laughed.

They approached the fourth generation of the Anti-Fascist Protection Rampart made from reinforced concrete and topped with smooth pipe. The Grenzmauer 75 or Border Wall dating to 1975. Adina looked up at a ten-sided circular watchtower with a square window on each side. The lookout post was perched on concrete cylinders stacked in sections. She thought there must be a circular staircase inside and noticed the outline of two border guards standing on top of the hut near the iron hand rail that ran around the roof.

They must have strange emotions, she thought, with their gate wide open. All gates are open now, she sang to herself—lyrics from a group in the west her mother knew about for some reason. Adina followed a long line of cars through the first chain link fence topped with barbed wire. The car rumbled over the metal grate of an anti-vehicle trench.

"West Berliners once dug a tunnel under these barriers and helped many people escape," Maria said.

"Those were brave souls." Beata looked up in the sky. "Lord have mercy on them."

Light from a powerful street lamp shone on the car. As they drew closer to the watchtower, Adina observed one policeman taking binoculars from another, adjusting the space between the barrels with gloved hands. He turned one of the eyepieces, then raised the binoculars and looked through them. His leather-clad hands covered his face in a V-shape and the lenses gave him bug eyes. With his belted overcoat and wool cap, he looked as though he had stepped out of a catalogue of military uniforms—Adina felt no nostalgia for this fashion or for men like Richard.

As she watched him, he covered one of the lenses with his hand, made an adjustment and then covered the other while turning one of the eyepieces. Then he trained the binoculars on her. She looked away.

"Do you see that, mother?" Adina pointed to the wall. "I don't understand how a man could balance on the smooth pipe atop the wall and juggle pins at the same time."

Beata looked in the back seat. "How about that, Maria? Did you ever think you would see people holding hands and dancing on top of the wall as soldiers stand around and do nothing?"

Adina felt as though the car was busting through the wall as it slowly rolled into swarms of pedestrians. She glanced out the side window and caught a glimpse of the wall from the west, for the first time. A ladder and its shadow were painted on it. A man was depicted pushing on the wall from the east with ghostly images of many others behind him, a tribute to the escapees and those who had died or had been injured trying to escape. The word überwinden or 'overcoming' was stenciled on the wall.

Adina drove smiling through the ebullient masses as they pounded on cars, raised fists, waved candles and sparklers. Shouts as simple as "one, two, three, hurrah." She caught a glimpse of the wall in her side-view mirror—at a painting of humans with symmetrical heads running on gears and waving flags. She hadn't known what to expect. She knew better but half-expected these westies to have typewriter cylinders coming out of their ears and cameras for eyes. They couldn't be like that if they make those paintings, she thought, and even though her cousins weren't like that, she had the impression people were somewhat mechanical in the west. She could now see with her own eyes they were wild as she slowed to a stop for a young man who stood in her way. He quickly walked to the windshield and kissed it. She rolled down the window.

"Why don't you kiss me instead of that glass?"

"Welcome to the west." He leaned inside the car and kissed her on the lips. "We need more women like you here."

"About that much I'm sure," Adina said.

He smiled at her.

Beata pulled on her daughter's right arm but he kissed her again and turned away.

"You have to be careful of germs," Beata said. "If he'll kiss your windshield, he'll kiss anything."

"I was hoping he'd kiss my ass," Adina said.

Maria laughed.

"Adina," Beata said in an admonishing tone.

Adina's senses surged in an orgy of color and chaos as though she had moved from the somber tone of a Rembrandt onto a canvas by Rubens. The unimaginable had happened, and unlike the public health parade, everyone—except the bewildered border guards crouching to examine the partially destroyed wall—wept tears of joy.

Adina had no idea where to go. Even if she had been inclined, she couldn't have studied the roads because West Berlin had been airbrushed off the socialist street map. Maria had been in the west the day the wall was constructed—she sneaked under the wire to be with her youngest daughter,

Beata. It had been so long, she scarcely remembered a thing about the west. Besides, everything had changed. Beata was the only one who had a vague idea where to go and what to do.

"Turn here," Beata said, also exhilarated by the noise and commotion. "Let's get out of this traffic jam. Why don't you park right away? We can walk from here."

Adina drove ahead a ways, over smooth roads. Around the bend lined with sleek office buildings, she pulled over and parked. The three women got out. Grandma was still in her pajamas, tipsy from beer, but that was fine today. They wove their way through the variegated masses, Beata leading the way back east, each carrying a beer.

"Look at this," Beata said.

People scaled the wall, leapt up and down, clinging to each other. Voices rose up from the crowd: "Sure are a hell of a lot of fucking people." "Honecker is a thinshit with farts in his brain." "The wall is the asshole of the earth."

Adina spun deliriously through a wild carousel of hugs. She sprung free from one man, wound around another, worked her way a few steps and flung her arms over another's shoulders. He shook her with a squeeze and she burst into tears. Together, they slipped and slid through beer puddles toward the wall. Every bump was forgiven, no caress forsaken, nothing forbidden. It was spring in fall. Adina gulped her beer as the sensation-hungry crowd swam through the night drunk on champagne bursting out of bottle after bottle—champagne they wore like sweat.

As they approached the wall, Adina spotted her father pecking away at it with his hammer and chisel. Never has he been so happy about hard work, she thought. Grandmother found her oldest daughter nearby—she was standing near other men as they too pecked away at the wall. A man grabbed

Adina's hands and danced her in circles until she became dizzy. Mother is trying to mount the wall, Adina noted, and when everything finally stopped spinning, she saw a hand slither under Beata's dress and push her up the concrete surface.

Then the hand changed its mind. The hand belonged to a member of Günter's work brigade who lowered her as if he didn't have the strength to hike her all the way up. He lowered her into his arms and dug his hands into the cloth of her panties. Beata's head fell back in lust, exposing her neck in a markedly vulnerable way—it had been so long.

Günter was oblivious as first one, then another of his fellow workers pulled at Beata's panties; others stepped in to block the husband's view. With a playful tug along her hip, the thin cloth unraveled a bit. Then one worker ripped her panties right off her rump and wore them like a crown. The others laughed as he ducked with a finger to his lips to be quiet while exaggeratedly looking between his fingers for Günter. Even Beata laughed. While others held her legs, the worker fingered her. She got loose and juicy right away. He extracted his fingers, now coated with her honey, and sucked them as other fingers filled the void.

They passed her around like a bottle of cheap wine, making trial caresses in a preamble before the real orgy began. Beata's ample breasts glowed in the moonlight—her dress was now a belt around her waist. Someone pushed her face up onto a bent-over worker, the one with her panties on his head, pushed her belly up onto his back. They steadied her thighs by holding them open while the biggest, drunkest, worst worker of the lot unbuckled his belt.

She moaned at the sight of the blue vein lines running the length of his shaft, the twitching shaft that jutted up from a tangle of curly black hair and swept into a flared head. With a shove from behind, he kneeled down and sank the darkly purple serrated rim of his cockhead into Beata's pink folds. For an instant, he paused, and then bucked in deep, then deeper, oozing in. The cheers from the crowd rang in her ears and she thrived on his rough bucking. Her cunt sucked him, her tits jiggled over her torso.

The vibrations concentrated in her throbbing pussy yet spread over her rocking belly and swaying breasts—the charges ran up and down her spine, still back to back with the jester who steadied herself with his hands on his knees. They held her by the ankles and bent her hips backwards as he rammed in and in between thighs spread wide like swan's wings. He sensed her first orgasms building. Her hands grabbed the asses of the other workers as he thrust into her bottom, digging her nails into them. She bathed his cock in hot juices as he hooked her legs over his shoulders.

"Pump it, baby, just pump it," Beata told him.

He gripped her tits as seed spouted from him, thick spurts in her hairy, dripping plug, which was still, despite her age, velvety in its sunken recesses. Beata clambered off the worker's back and, looking up at the man, fell to her knees. So well had she learned the meanings of the KuV credo that she sought to make things grow from below—she licked and sucked her juices off the long, thick cock while rubbing it against her face.

"If Günter could see you now," he said.

"He can have some too if he wants." She pulled the cock back. "It's not every day the wall comes down."

"It's not every day we get to fuck the wife of my boss," the worker who had been her bed said. "Share the favors, why don't you?"

His prick sprang forth, right in her face. She turned to it and feasted on the end of this stand still held in the palm of his hand. Flashing sensations ran through his body as her lips enveloped him. She drank deeper, pulling on him rhythmically. She ran her tongue down the shaft, to his scrotum, and inched one of his plum-sized nuts into her mouth and then silently pledged devotion to his bottom. Instantly drunk from the initial taste, she paused to prepare herself to sink her tongue up the worker's steaming rectum. At that instant, Adina's gaze stared back at Beata in disbelief.

Adina wobbled, wavered. She fell back a bit into arms covered by black leather. Drops of water fell on her face. Her eyes closed for an instant. Water cannons from the East blasted people off the wall. Albert, the man who held Adina up by her balcony, slipped the bottle of beer out of her fingers and leaned against the wall. Adina looked up at the handsome man with curly blond hair who was drinking her beer, then another man fell from the wall to the ground next to them—he dusted himself off with a groan. She turned back and smiled at Albert.

This was her first encounter with a westie and it seemed glamorous. An inner storm brewed inside her, she trembled in his arms. He took a long drink from her bottle.

"You must have fainted," Albert said over the noise from the crowd.

"Yes, my mother . . . my family. Where are they?"

"I don't know."

"The excitement must have been too much for me," she said.

"Take it easy for a moment. You're as pale as stone."

She held her head in her hands.

"My name is Albert, you?"

"Adina."

"You're the one."

"What?"

Albert had come to the wall to look for eastern women. As a film director, he wanted to capture the moment and experience his west through the eyes of the other. Easties were his brothers and sisters, but he, like many others, had somehow thought they were weaker. How could these people have treated each other with socialist cruelty he wondered, or stood for it? How will the west affect them? He hoped to exploit the difference on film by capturing an alien in his city . . . she seemed sensitive, perhaps a special case who had a psychological dimension to her beauty. As for Adina's beauty—she dazzled him, and she knew it.

"I want to give you a kiss for catching me," Adina said.

He closed his eyes and moved toward her. Lips met in a moist, engulfing kiss. He held her like that for a moment, inhaling her country sweetness. She tilted her chin upward, her eyes holding his like an actress. They kissed again and their lips articulated a victory over fear and paranoia, hello kisses and the coming together of brother and sister. The unspoken language of instinctual responses between their legs, bittersweet tears trickling over their lips.

Adina, half-oblivious, nonetheless sensed her libidinal capital rise as he responded to her. She flowed into him with her hips, willingly testing the effectiveness of well-practiced moves. The love lines of a leading lady, he thought. For her, it was as if her beauty-of-the-Linden large breasts and long legs had more value in the west.

"I think," Albert said wiping away first his tears, then hers, "you are the one who caught me."

Adina fingered his leather jacket and she looked down, at his crotch. "You know, I've never been able to come to the west. This is my first time."

She had forgotten her family and was somewhat worried this was a dream. If the wall closed up again like a tomb, she didn't know what she would do.

"Didn't you want to come over the wall?"

"Sure. It's just that . . ." Adina thought of Richard. "I could never get a visa."

"Allow me to give you a tour. What do you want to see?"

"Everything."

"I'll show you everything, take you anywhere you want to go, but you must promise to act in a film for me." He pulled out a paper. "I have a contract."

"You want me to be an actress?"

"Yes."

"What does it say?" Adina asked.

"Read it if you like. It's a standard contract. I've left compensation blank for the moment. Let's just say that I'll cover your expenses and we'll talk about money later. We should enjoy the moment."

Adina didn't hesitate—she would be in his movie if he wanted, why not? And she would get paid for it or else have Richard enforce the contract.

"I'll do it," she said with a smile.

He turned and she signed the contract on the back of his black leather jacket.

# CHAPTER 5

Jan, the Polish clerk from the State Hotel, took in the young people outside the anarchist bookshop in the West Berlin neighborhood of Kreuzberg in the low light of dusk. He correctly surmised they were the ones he had read about in underground journals that were smuggled over the wall: a mix of students from the Freie Universität—home to Red Army Faction sympathizers, anarchists and radical feminists—along with unemployed youth living in cold-water, semi-abandoned flats around Gropius City—clean, geometric, predictable housing for the ones who withdrew their obedience from work—Redskins, Blackskins and Mohicans with their half-shaved heads and torn leather jackets.

Jan knew from someone with firsthand experience, a westie, that these kids often came to the neighborhood where Turks and radicals lived in relative harmony to the anarchist meeting spot A-Laden, a shop that opened every now and then when there was something to discuss. He could tell some came from the drug and music underworld by the fashionable boredom they exuded, by their nose studs, facial tattoos and other forms of self-mutilated chic.

He watched in the dim light from across the street as they came on motorcycles with bandanas pulled over their faces to a door between shuttered storefronts or on foot with tee shirts under leather jackets. A small crowd gathered to buy pretzels from a Turk with a wicker basket on his bicycle.

There was not much to see, especially as the atmosphere darkened, but Jan knew there were some good books in there— ones he would not be able to find elsewhere. Off to the side of the shop, in front of the closed store, young people squatted and inspected used clothes in an impromptu flea market run by a guy sitting on a plastic chair chained to a drainpipe. Others were standing nearby, talking and smoking around bicycles locked to an old iron light pole with ornate molding.

As Jan turned to leave, intending to come back another time, a heavy-set, dark-haired woman crossed his path wearing a "Work, No Thanks" tattoo on her forehead.

"Hello," Jan said.

She walked by without responding, her attention focused on the top copy of a stack of leaflets, and belatedly turned back to extend a leaflet to Jan.

"Oh, I'm sorry," she said. "We're going to the east—you should come."

Jan smiled. "I already live there."

"We'll see you on the other side."

As she crossed the street and greeted some of the people outside the shop, Jan glanced down at the leaflet and began to walk away. Der schwarze block[17], Jan thought, the ones who want to turn the east from red to black.

---

[17]    The black bloc.

Jutte smiled as she passed out a hastily photocopied leaflet to the twenty-odd people there inside the shop, thanking them for coming. A young woman squeezed through the crowd at the door and accepted the paper without apprehension or smug appraisal of the tattoo across Jutte's forehead or her lip ring. Once inside, the young woman took off her jacket—her Good Women Go to Heaven; Bad Women Go to Berlin tee shirt drew smiles from people milling amid book bins filled with Bakunin, Kropotkin, Stirner, Spooner, Berkman, Traven, Malatesta and others, including Vaneigem; they gazed at the magazine racks and banners on the ceiling, smoking under a painting of Honecker and Brezhnev friendship kissing in the nude.

They knew Jutte's tattoo was a reaction to the compulsory obsequiousness demanded by postmodern economies, but it applied to conventional forms of labor too—the forced discipline of a traditional prison-factory that recalled the infamous Arbeit Macht Frei[18] slogan over the entrance to a Nazi concentration camp. But when she turned her back to the recipients of her leaflets, she heard real or imagined laughter behind her.

Was Jutte laughable? Yes and no. Perhaps it was her Adolf Hitler, European Tour 1939 (Austria, Czechoslovakia, Poland, etc.) tee shirt or her tragic lack of beauty or her notorious frustration with the opposite sex. On the other hand, without her dynamism, they wouldn't be there—she brought them together with her supportive efforts and soft speech.

"Can I get some quiet, please?" Jutte held up her hands.

"Thanks. I'm sure you've heard the big news—the wall is open."

---

[18]    Work Makes One Free.

"Yyyyeaaahhyeyeyaaaaaaoowwww!!!"

"I appreciate you coming here tonight. Most of you, I'm sure, would rather party in the street with everyone else."

"What did you say?" A rap assassin, already half-deaf from his own music, cupped his ear.

"We're here because some of us see the chaos created by the opening of the wall as a great opportunity. Sure, we have our conflicts. But what excites me tonight is what unifies us, namely the desire to create different living conditions with as much self-determination as we can muster and our solidarity against growing racism, neofascism and police-state measures."

"We can be heroes," a skinny punk yelled from the back of the room.

"As the leaflet says," Jutte continued, "we know there are over twenty-five thousand vacant apartments in East Berlin. Mainzerstrasse is probably the best location. It's up to you, but many of us feel that tonight is the night to act. With the euphoria and chaos, we will move into buildings. Those of you who want to take part might bring food, tools and weapons in caravans of no more than four people, so we don't attract attention."

A handsome Turk raised a bottle of wine. With his black hair combed back and thick, broad mustache spreading across his face as he spoke, he was a perfect parody of a postage stamp portrait of comrade Stalin, only with darker skin and flashing eyes.

"I'm so glad," he began, translating roughly from the big print of a book from the Belgian writer they all liked so much, "that I, the ghost of Stalin, am here when my German children are at last reconciled. History has finally exhausted its genres with this east-west vaudeville, as I've commented regarding this painting of Brezhnev and Honecker. My case, as you know, was tragic. The world favored bourgeois dramas starring the most docile workers the world has ever known—consumers. Unfortunately, we never went from production communism to consumption communism. But the current producers should be careful, lest these vaudevilles catch on and everyone wants democracy. So many actors like Reagan and Gorbachev come and go, they cast their shadows on scenes that use the red flag for a setting sun."

"Thank you Hadid," Jutte said. "The sun may be setting on your lovely performance."

"Don't underestimate my weight in the balance of history," he added, knowing she would let him get in a few last words, "because a cadaver with self-respect eats the living without chattering its teeth."

Jutte smiled, happy to have the support of this tall foreigner. Hadid was a decadent pessimist who also affected western ways in subtle but cruel parodies of western values. Obligatory black leather jacket and fashionable white jeans, new used clothes worn with studious spontaneity hinting at Third World origins. This was Hadid's silent response to the Kraut with short dreadlocks and a reggae tee shirt. Jutte and the other women in their circle couldn't understand Hadid, though many tried. They fell for his striking features—lustrous hair, thick eyebrows, deep eyes and a strong, chiseled chin. But his foreignness mesmerized them more than anything, it mystified them. He seemed confident, even if his German and Turkish halves didn't know one another very well. With his Stalin pranks and drinking, it seemed to the women that he had risen above the world in a personal insurrection that came from who knows where, as if being a stranger to himself gave him a radical sense of sovereignty.

Of all their comrades who championed Third World and other causes, Hadid came closest to embodying his origins with ancestral grace, especially when he danced. He was, with his unselfconscious movements, what escaped them and what they escaped in themselves, despite their feminist anthropology and tattoos. He joined Jutte as she spoke with small groups, filling them in on the events and planned actions. He was agreeing with her with his eyes and head gestures while drinking wine from a bottle in a paper bag.

He noticed how clusters had formed: post-punkers in black bombers who had reconciled themselves to rock, writers of Berlin scenester literature, bad women with brazen beauty, ecosluts with dyed green hair and blue nails, others with white berets and skimpy sheaths, and then the ones who were notorious for their orgiastic capacity during sexual warfare. Many still clung to militant forms of discourse while exceeding the simplicities of ceremonial transgression. They gave themselves with insatiable freedom and without a trace of prudish submission or hysterics. Their sex was rather cool, ostensibly free of jealousy and private passion. One took a pull on Hadid's bottle; another stood on her tiptoes and licked his mustache.

"Come with us, Hadid."

"Thanks." He flashed a sly grin. "But I'll see you there. I think I should go with Jutte."

They would want him to party all night and come five times as if it were a categorical imperative. He could handle two, three times, sure, but no more. He was no longer young.

"As you like . . ." the other young woman, the one who licked him, said over her shoulder.

Hadid was a group of one, highly conscious of meeting his internal other—the one he seemed to be at times, as if a stranger in a bar. These chance meetings gave shape to Hadid, a fuzzy-shaped set of active nihilism, indomitable absurdity and personal anarchy. He was also loyal. As Jutte passed through the tangle of bodies, Hadid grabbed her elbow.

"Let's go."

Jutte smiled, pleasantly surprised, and followed him out with the others. The shuffle of heavy boots in the night, maybe a hundred or more, moving straight ahead, sideways, down obscure passageways—urban guerrillas advancing street by street: Manteuffelstrasse, Oranienstrasse, Heinrich-Heine-Strasse past Karl Liebknecht Library. They mostly dressed in black and gray to chromatically blend with the night. Veils of steam from a grate . . . ubiquitous graffiti: FUCK THE LAW, BUS AND TRAIN FOR FREE, SHELL TO HELL SCHNELL[19], DIE AUTONOME GRUPPE . . .

They took vans, cars, motorcycles with sidecars; they wheeled bicycles into subway cars and regrouped in the vacant lot at the end of an elevated pedestrian walk, not far from Checkpoint Charlie. Kids sitting on suitcases, on rocks, amid puddles. They huddled for a few moments then moved on, marching over the open border and catching trams in the east. Some had never voyaged on these electrified glass ships that now resembled giant toys on their iron tracks given the playful nature of their expedition.

Hadid nodded to a gray-bearded Turk taking down his fruit stand as they neared Jutte's car.

"I'll drive," he offered.

"Okay."

Hadid's duffel bag and a few of her things were already stuffed in the front seat of her Volkswagen. Jutte squeezed her

---

[19]   Fast or in a hurry.

hefty frame in back. Hadid leaned forward and turned the key. The car sputtered to life. He turned and arched his eyebrow.

"All right, lady, where to?"

"To the east," Jutte said. "I'm so excited. Not just by the opening, we'll make it happen. What should we call it? The Alternative?"

Hadid silently pulled on his wine as he drove, then replaced the bottle with a cigarette. As he exhaled, he flicked his ashes out a crack in the window. He slowed. Figures in the fog crossed the street. They passed. He drove on and time slowed, grew more palpable, as more alcohol coursed through his veins, cutting the oxygen to his brain. The car pulled up to a light. In the Mercedes next to him, a huge dog in the passenger seat stared at them.

Hadid drove on with Jutte in the back. She was so excited she couldn't help herself. Her hand fumbled under the folds of her dress, the hairy folds, as gleaming steel and glass buildings flashed by. If she could, she would put an end to the world of sex. Few lesbians would touch her, as much as she liked them. She was liked as a person, but that wasn't enough; she loved the way she loved herself, with her incomparable narcissism that was the result of the hatred she felt when she looked in the mirror. The more she analyzed herself, the faster she masturbated, her fingers clawing in a frenzy like fluttering leaves on the trees lining the sidewalk as vehicles went by.

Jutte inhaled a whiff of Hadid's smoke, the Turkish tobacco that had passed through his body. Ashes fluttered over her. She opened her legs wider to the aroma of wine and Hadid's pungent body oils. Her hair grew thicker and kinkier up her inner thighs, at the hot point where her legs joined. The hairs shimmered in intervals as the street lights passed, hairs wet with the moisture conducted by her palm as she rubbed the full length of her blooming vulva.

Jutte gripped her inner thighs from underneath, digging her fingers into her folds. She lurched forward as if trying to catch Hadid, but all she got was a slit full of air. She sucked in her breath sharply and moved her right hand back into the soup that was drowning her bearded lower mouth.

If those lips could speak, Hadid said to himself as he listened to them smack in hunger for him. He leaned a little into a left-hand turn and glanced out his passenger side window. What would those lips say? Feed me fingers, fists, feed me anything, but what I wouldn't do for a cock. He chuckled quietly, knowing she wanted him to shame her.

"Should I get out?" Hadid asked as he watched her contorted face in the rearview mirror.

"No, no . . . go on."

She quivered a little all over her body, coming right on the back seat.

# CHAPTER 6

Adina's perfect skin lost its color as they moved—she and Albert—out of the shadow of the wall. She staggered away from him with a slack-jawed look of shock. He was unaware she had just watched her mother actually finish the man from her father's construction brigade and wipe her chin clean with the back of her hand. Adina vowed to abolish the image from her mind—there would be no going back.

Albert pulled her waist. "How about a coffee?"

He took her silence for a yes, this narcissistic director, so tall, blond and good-looking—a man made for women like her who return love, accept hospitality and expect to become stars. They stopped under the awning of an imbiss stand.

"Two coffees with brandy," Albert said.

The pudgy, balding proprietor, preoccupied with hot dogs, nodded, glancing up for an instant. Albert needed coffee to stay wide awake for Adina's one-shot film—the one he was making in his mind with no edits about her impressions of otherwise familiar images. These new-because-of-her images could partially satisfy the director's hopeless fetish. But the image of a middle-aged woman, her mother, on her hands and knees in public, sucking a fat one, came back to Adina as the proprietor handed out sausages to other customers. Adina pulled her purse higher on her shoulder, looked away from the stand in the direction they came. She hoped her grandmother fared well, and then she again imagined her mother doing those terrible things.

She closed her eyes as it dawned on her that from the moment Adina arrived in the west, she faced the supersaturation of the eyes by images: shadows of heels under a streetlamp; zebra stripes on iron pylons; runaways loitering near benches; an old man listening to music from a miniature hand organ, the sound muffled by earmuffs, a cane over his forearm; laughter down a blind alley.

Albert handed her the steaming drink. "How does it feel to be in the west?" He motioned toward the counter.

She set her drink down. "What do you mean, 'How does it feel?' I feel fine. Sure I've been drinking beer, but I don't want you to think I'm intoxicated by your billboards and shop windows. I've seen it on the tele. Life probably isn't so different in my Berlin."

"There must be something new for you." He rubbed her back. "Have you ever been to a casino?"

Adina smiled wearily. "Never."

"My casino never closes."

He hailed a cab. Albert's accumulated experiences and libidinal capital prepared him well for her. She could have her pick: cafés, boutiques, cabarets—anything, if she did as he asked. How could she refuse? What if she refused? The cab slid through the fluid hyperspace of Kurfürstendamm, or Ku'damm as locals call the expansive avenue with its jewelry stores, restaurants, big city lights on high rise buildings—flashing neon and digital signs—like constellations around the revolving Mercedes star atop the giant Europa Center.

Whenever he was looking at the city through glass like this, riding in a car, he was reminded of a pop-rock song about a passenger who is a little bored and looks up at the hollow sky. He wanted to tell her about the throaty drum and clanging of the guitars in such a catchy beat, but he sensed she wouldn't understand. Adina surged with euphoria as she moved through this world that still seemed distant. Her eyes widened; everything seemed unreal, like images on a screen or seen through the lens of a tourist's camera.

However wide the angle, she knew she was missing something. She felt alien here and tried to unify her senses with the west, so she cleaved to Albert.

"What if I told you," she said looking up at him, "you could have everything?"

He caressed her shoulder, her neck—every touch was a stroke on the kaleidoscopic painting going on in her mind.

"What are you doing?"

"You're my actress, you know?" Albert whispered in her ear as he nibbled on her neck.

"What role have you cast me in?"

"A passenger from the east."

"Ha," she laughed.

He ran his hand up her thigh, over her hip and continued up, lingering on her jutting nipples.

"In this part, you must translate your pride and confidence into a cold, even cruel, form of indifference."

Adina removed his hand from her breast.

"That's it, as you wish," Albert continued, "and if you can make me happy doing it, I'll give you whatever you want."

His head fell back, as if enacting his fantasies in his mind.

She examined him closely. What does he mean, she thought, by "that's it"? He's always on about *it* . . . like how does it feel . . . and doing it. I don't get it, it's almost as if this 'it' is the subconscious they always told us the west would penetrate. Maybe they were right. She pictured herself as a cinematic, celluloid woman in hot lights on a cold screen—the liquid flow of scenes of her in a luxurious room as they passed the male whores near Zoo Station, one runaway with his dog and bottle, and farther on, a gaggle of runaways. The taxi sped away.

Albert pointed to a nondescript restaurant named after a German philosopher. "Where spies meet. You know, I was thinking about doing a movie on the so-called walkers, the low-level agents sent back and forth across the border."

The taxi pulled up to a light as she listened distractedly.

"It would've been a conceptual movie with people receiving messages to appear at a set time and place, say, at this Hegel Bar."

She turned back toward him, looking out the window.

"An agent could watch you, for example, sitting in the window and talk about how your appearance tells him you're ready for work—a film watching him watch you watching to see if you're under surveillance."

"We could film in the east too," she said. "Now that the wall is down."

Albert nodded. "And at parties, where you will actually meet important industrialists and officials willing to play a small part in the film."

"You sound like a voyeur," she said.

The cab dropped them curbside in front of a steel and glass skyscraper. They walked a few feet and Albert quietly slipped behind her in the revolving door and orchestrated a dizzy kiss as they spun inside. She had big juicy lips that left a lingering sensation on his.

They stepped into a mirrored corridor, their reflection in the walls projected on the ceiling. Adina looked up to see herself. A door opened and a couple walked through it, into a wall of sound blasting from the simulated jungle lounge inside—bodies in mute expression on the dance floor, seen for an instant as they walked by.

The elevator arrived, occupied by people coming up from the garage. Adina shuddered at the withered skin on the faces of the ruling class. Too much rich food and strong drink, Adina thought as they climbed the elevator shaft. What good is this wealth, these fast cars and this pseudosophistication? I imagine they like losing money until five in the morning so they can grow old too soon. In the elevator, a tux and a low-cut silk dress . . . sequins, double strands of pearls in sagging cleavage, powdered blond hair. What did they say? That I'm Polish? They don't think I understand. And think of the west's poverty, unemployment, racism—did I say racism? Yes, racism and violence, at least on the news and in the movies. If I'm a little like that, others must be much worse.

The elevator reached the top and Albert guided her to a nearby window. The view of the east, unlike the west, was censored by buildings. How different is he from them? Adina thought of Albert and the procession of wealthy hedonists filing by. We have more discipline in the east. Our struggle makes us stronger. I'll get Albert in line, the problem is, he'll probably like it. That was it.

"So how do you like it?" Albert asked with an expansive wave out the window, as if he could reap the marketing myths of West Berlin.

"I'll learn to like it just fine. You were taking me to the casino?"

He motioned her inside, holding the small of her back as they skimmed over the floor. Adina's expectations were dashed by the mechanical sound of one-armed bandits and mediocre men—mustachioed dealers and croupiers who were nothing like those water ball men. She watched the roulette wheel and her mind drifted to her mother on her knees.

"This place gives me the creeps," Adina said.

"Let's go then."

They turned together.

"I don't need to get my gambling juices going anyway," Albert said. "But tell me, what don't you like?"

"I just don't like it."

Outside Europa Center, Adina panned left and right, watching humans loitering near the zoo and estimating their price and proclivities. Albert watched her for a second, then he led her away, under a pedestrian overpass.

"Wait," she said.

Albert took her in his leather-covered arms and kissed her, lifting her off the ground and twirling her around.

"Put me down," Adina said.

Albert set her down.

"Where are we going?"

Albert stroked his chin in mock thought. "Why not go back to Hegel Bar? It's just around the corner, on Kantstrasse."

They took a few steps.

"Most of the spies our people take there are Russians pretending to be Germans—double agents."

"I don't like Russians. You're not a spy, are you?"

"No, I told you. I'm a film director."

He pointed to the green and red neon sign PARIS BAR. "I could take you there."

"I'll tell you where I want to go."

"Where?"

"There."

She pointed to a sex shop.

Albert swallowed hard. Not what he'd expected, but he didn't know what to expect. Why not? he thought. There's probably not much of a sex industry in the east and she's curious what it's like. With his arm behind her back, they strode over to the shop and he ushered her in. Adina first noticed the fleshy jowls of an old man bent over a book, near the cash register. Men of many ages looked at video titles: Suck, Café, Flesh, Take It Off and so on. Other than the blow-up fuck doll, Adina was the only woman in the store. She strolled over to the dildo display. One reminded her of Richard, only there was no danger to these lifeless rows of disembodied sex machines.

Albert moved behind her, whispered in her ear. "Let's see a video."

With a fistful of tokens, Albert led Adina through a curtain into a dimly lit arcade, past booths with little marquees: Berlin Without a Blouse, Dachau Sex Slave, She-Wolf of the SS. The arcade was full of tourists looking for the long-lost Berlin experience and porn addicts in search of a sexual fix. Adina held his hand and followed him as they started into a cabin built for one. A tall Berliner vied with Albert for a booth.

"Go ahead," the man said with a civic tone, "and let me have a go with her when you're done, eh?"

"Fuck off."

"Let's see this one," Adina whispered.

Albert locked the door as the camera faded into a dark, dank room—shot from outside, looking in a basement window. Pan along the wall: sink, towel rack, wardrobe, sleeping dog, nightstand, bed—in the foreground, a round table and three chairs.

## LUSTMORD (SEX MURDER)

The door to the basement apartment opens. A female sex worker, large and bloated, strolls in, followed by a desperate man with clenched teeth. His large nose, small eyes, sloping forehead and sperm stains cast suspicion.

"Make yourself at home," the sex worker says with the accent of a prole who has bourgeois affectations.

"I'll do that," he replies in an acidic voice.

He sits at the table, while taking off his shoes.

The sex worker lays back in bed. "Now let me see your bone." She raises her dress, revealing a thick bush. "Come on, come and get it."

He looks at her strangely and gets up; his eyes dart around the room. She lowers her dress off her shoulders. Enormous breasts emerge.

"Or would you like an appetizer first?"

He moves to the sink and grabs a paring knife. The pine floor creaks as he turns.

"I'll eat you piece by piece." He throws himself on her. "Until there's nothing left of you but blood and guts, you sick, ugly whore. You gave me a disease."

"I've never seen you before," she says.

She tries to move off him; she does and inches back toward the wall. Body parts fly in a rain of blood that was reminiscent for Albert of what he remembered from a painting of a sex crime cavern in a the cathedral of erotic misfortune. And after his crime, the john smokes a cigar with his blood-soaked fingers while playing solitaire under a naked bulb, his lips stained red from the bottle of raspberry wine on the table. On the pine floor, the bloody knife. The camera pans to the bed: the remains of the sex worker draped over the edge, her throat slit. Pan out the basement window to a constellation of low-class apartment buildings made of scarred red brick.

Adina gasped. "Let's see something nicer."

She led him out of the booth.

Albert pointed to another. "How about this?"

They entered another booth; the token landed with a clink. The film was in mid-reel: orgasmic shrieks and sobs dubbed over a wide-angle, close-up of a cock plunging into a hairless cunt. Albert licked her ear.

"Lick this." Adina raised her dress and looked over her shoulder. "Go ahead."

Albert fell to his knees and pulled down her panties with his teeth. He added his saliva to the moisture of Adina's cunt with loving tongue strokes.

"I want to shave my cunny like her." Adina's eyes focused on the screen. "So you can lick me better." She pulled open her buns. "Lick my asshole, little dog . . . oh, that's it."

Albert's tongue slid over her rectum and fucked her ass.

"Suck it harder. Get it clean. Your nose will be in there in a minute."

Scarcely able to see the screen over Adina's wobbling buttocks, Albert made a movie in his mind, first half-drowning in wombwater while laughing at the distortion of the wide-angle lens and the dubious dubbing typical of porn. He felt her hand on his head and everything turned black as his eyes pressed into her buns. She liked the way his nose was rubbing into her asshole. No, Adina wasn't laughing, or if she was, it was at Albert now that she had him at her beck and call.

Grabbing his hair, she pulled his face from her deep cleavage. His cheeks were red and his chin glistened with juice.

"I want it good and hard," she said. "Can you do that?"

Albert nodded and moved behind her, the sound of his trousers sliding down to his ankles, a whisper in the darkness. Adina felt his cock prod between her cheeks, then slide down to her moist juncture. Albert groaned as he pushed inside while clawing her rump, the flesh spilling over his long fingers. He gasped in the tiny cabin and gave her quick thrusts that slowed as he filled her deeper. Her prick-grasping cunt was pumping back, enjoying his cock sliding in and out, all along her tight tunnel wall. The warmth of her pussy and the hot cabin air. She pushed him back with her butt, rearing him into the door, urging him to use greater force. He lurched forward, her cheeks slapped against his belly, his hands held her smooth hips, pulling and pushing her over his prick. At that moment, the token-activated timer ran out.

"Put in more money," Adina said, almost oblivious to the fact that Albert was inside her, that his pants were around his ankles.

Albert fell out of her juicy pussy as he dug for tokens in his pockets.

"Hurry," Adina urged.

Fumbling in the dark, Albert dropped six tokens into the slot, illuminating the booth with the variable light of the video.

"Oh, yeah," Adina gushed as Albert resumed pumping her.

She mimicked the dubbed groans of the porn star while thinking of Richard and of shaving her cunt so he would look bigger in the mirror. Adina rubbed her clit and the pressure on his cock relaxed with a flush of liquid. Albert quickened his pace. She matched him with moans, softer now, but sounding loud as the film ended. More strokes in dim light, three, four and Albert injected her with love.

A knock on the door.

"Hurry up," a man said in East Berlinerish. "We've got a line out here."

"What are you doing?" Albert asked Adina. "Wait for me."

She pushed Albert out the door and smiled at the next patron, a burly, big-toothed worker. Naked breasts dangled from her open dress. Albert reached for the hem of her dress, but she turned, brushing him aside and her rump against the worker's crotch. The sickly snickers of porn addicts in line fell on Albert's ears.

After some time, the worker came out first, followed by Adina.

"That wasn't in our contract," Albert snorted as the GDR worker pushed past him with a malicious grin, shoving his superior cock into his trousers.

"The what?" Adina asked. "Oh, yes. The contract. I only gave him a blowjob."

Exiting the booth, she smoothed out her dress in a way that highlighted the curve of her hips.

"I'll show you," Albert pulled out the paper. "It says that regardless of what transpires between us, you are never, I repeat never, to humiliate me in public."

"What good is it to humiliate you if I can't do it in public?" Adina asked.

Adina and Albert walked in front of a row of rubber lingerie, then out of the sex shop.

"You might—"

"Like it," she said, completing his thought with a mischievous smile that Albert found strangely reassuring.

Albert flagged a cab—they piled in and the car took off through the canyon of brick and glass buildings.

His fingers laced through hers. "What is your passion?"

"Passion?"

"In life."

"I love my family and my dog. But I never really knew passion until . . ."

"What?"

She shook her head and looked out the window. The cab dropped them at a renovated condo with an art deco awning, decorative pilasters tacked to the facade, a bust of Wagner in the gated garden. As Adina and Albert walked to the door, a businessman with trench coat and briefcase walked by, followed by a woman wearing an extravagant fur coat. A pile of cinderblocks on the sidewalk. Upscale Schöneberg, with its antiquitäten[20], Japan Basar and a young mother wheeling a baby carriage.

"You'll find certain advantages to being my actress," Albert said as he punched the security code, hastening to add, "beyond the fact that I will do whatever I can to give you pleasure."

"Give me pleasure?"

They stepped into the lobby.

"Yes." Albert led her toward the elevator. "Your pleasure is my pleasure."

The elevator opened, they moved into the wood-paneled compartment. Adina glared into his soft blue eyes.

"You're the director," she said, "and I'm the only passenger along for the ride."

He formed a camera frame with his thumbs and fingers and ogled her from various positions. She laughed along with

---

[20]     Antique shops.

this self-assured man who had been bold enough to start one of the many New German Film co-ops and finagle television coproduction money. They stepped out of the elevator.

"Go on ahead."

He motioned for her to walk down the hall, then framed his fingers again, drunk on the image of her and feeling foolish for it.

"You'll have to excuse the mess."

He opened the door on a flat that reflected relative success propagating the ideology of visibility. The inevitable photographs and pop art on off-white walls. Pillows lay scattered on an oriental carpet in the center of a spacious room. Consumerist kitsch (plastic shark, lobster, dinosaur, suction-tip arrow) and electronic gear were strewn about. She noticed a golf bag containing a quiver of riding crops. Spider plants spiraled toward the windows. Dark windows were dotted with distant streetlights.

She moved over to the golf bag and felt the crops for a lingering moment, then picked up the bag and put it on her shoulder.

"Allow me," he said.

"Not yet." She headed toward his bedroom, turned at the door. "This is now what you westies call the east, the forbidden room. You're not to enter without my permission. Understand?"

"You forbid me from entering my own bedroom?"

"Yes."

Adina slammed the door behind her.

Alone in Albert's room, she threw the bag of crops on the bed and rummaged through his closet, feeling the fabric of his suits, sniffing his tennis shoes. His tennis rackets and balls were stacked next to swimming equipment—goggles, kickboard, fins. So he's a country club boy. She tried on his rubber swim cap. It would help if I wet my hair, she thought. She moved to the bathroom, opened the medicine cabinet. Hmmm, Vademecum. I like it, she said to herself as she read the toothpaste ingredients: chamomile, mint, rosemary. I'll use his toothbrush, then take a bath and make him wait.

As an afterthought, Adina set Albert's shaving kit on the edge of the tub, along with his nose hair scissors. She eased out of her dress as the tub filled with steaming water while admiring her vapor-veiled form in the mirror. One leg followed another, then her languid body eased into the voluptuous liquid. Ah, I could stay here forever, she thought as she sank in deeper and deeper, up to her mouth. The spray nozzle sprang to life at her touch and snaked away underwater. She caught it and aimed it at the semen Albert had deposited in her at the sex shop. It felt good and she kept it there for several delicious moments, playing the videos over in her mind.

Humming to herself, she moved her soap-slick butt up to the edge of the tub. Goosebumps sprouted on her shoulders and arms as she gathered her pubes in her fingers and clipped them with the scissors. After a few more ceremonial snips, she lathered her mons with shaving cream and scraped the hair around her lower lips. She pulled first one, then a second disposable razor over the tender flesh with short, precise strokes, leaning forward, taking pains not to cut herself. The pulsating nozzle washed the cuttings away. She lathered the remaining patches closest to her labia again and finished with a third razor.

The water, less warm as she eased in this time, still felt good, especially with the pulsing spray nozzle against her hairless snatch. Her head tilted backwards, dipping into the bathwater. She found Albert's natural sponge in the rack next to the tub and floated it between her protuberant breasts. Her slender hands fingered his rich, fragrant soaps. The lather and sponge sensation on her arm and shoulder sent new shivers up her spine. She abandoned the sponge and lay back in the tub. Her eyes blinked shut and open again as the swimcap formed a bond with her scalp. She noticed the rubber hose attached to the spray nozzle.

"That's it," she said out loud.

She rose from the bath and with a heavy towel dabbed the sweat on her forehead, then her body. She pushed a few stray hairs under the swim cap. With the water off, the white rubber hose sank limply to the bottom of the draining tub. Adina bent at the waist and reached across to the faucet. She cut the hose using Albert's nose hair scissors. The spray nozzle dripped into the empty tub. What more? I know, she said to herself as she put a foot on the toilet and smeared lip rouge over her labia.

Armed with the hose, water still dripping off her tits, Adina stormed into the living room where Albert set his video camera on a tripod. The monitor rolled Bronson in Der Liquidator— zoom from the depths of a room to a close-up of the actor's elastoplast face intercut with blurred, slowmotion shots of guns firing and corpses on the floor. Adina whipped the hose, aiming for his back. She missed and smacked his neck. Albert winced in pain, then switched the video camera on by remote.

Hearing the camera click on, Adina slowly turned on her toe and winked at the lens—she flayed Albert again, this time hitting him across the back. He yelped and cringed in pain as a gust of heat seared him.

"Strip for me," Adina commanded.

Albert watched her out of the corner of his eye as he took off his clothes. Adina bent over, and with a rocking motion, touched her toes several times, blowing kisses to the camera, intently looking backwards between her legs at the lens. Her lower lips flamed with lipstick, her taut buttocks swayed and muscles rippled up and down her long legs as she stretched one leg, then another.

Raising up she took the hose over her head—she turned and stretched her shoulders so that her breasts protruded in profile before the lens. The swim cap, rubber hose and calisthenics gave her the look of an alien sex queen or space age Amazon. Albert looked on, nude on the floor, his head tilted up at her.

"Get on all fours."

Albert complied. Adina looked at the camera as if it were a person, say, an unmasked Stasi agent. She turned back to Albert.

"No, not like that, you idiot. Turn this way so the camera can document the growth of the welts I'm giving you."

The hose cracked close to Albert's scrotum, his balls shrank. Adina whipped the hose across the back of his legs— dangerously close to his genitals. He remained on all fours as she loosened up for a moment. I'll put more into this whack, she thought. She cracked the hosetip on his nuts. Take that. Tears streamed down his face; she hit him again and he yelped like a wounded dog.

"Spineless cur," Adina grunted under her breath. She thought of Richard, of what she'd been taught to believe real men did with women. "That's what I want." She pointed to Bronson on television. "But you can't give it to me, can you?"

"No," Albert gritted through his teeth.

"No? No, what?"

"No . . ." He shied away from *fräulein* and amended it in his mind. "*Frau* . . ."

He wanted to add her last name, but he didn't know it.

"Schulte," she said, adding, "And don't forget it. You should have seen it on the contract. Can't you read?"

Adina whipped him twice, hard, very hard. "Roll over so I can see your cock."

She ignored his obvious excitement, slowly lowering her painted lower lips over his mouth and blowing kisses to the camera. With her free hand, she opened her cheeks and worked her rectum over the tip of his nose.

"Where is it? There," she said to no one as she snuggled into position.

She rocked on her giant seahorse, spurring him on with the rubber hose. If there were a split screen, the side representing Albert's perspective would be black. Adina's taut buttocks pressed, with the full weight of her statuesque body, on his eyes. Her thighs cupped his ears like seashells, making sounds reminiscent of waves on a windy beach as she rocked to and fro. His nostrils pinched shut in the grip of her powerful sphincter and he was drowning in pussy juice. His lungs flinched in pain.

She'll suffocate me, he thought as she leaned forward, moving her pussy to where her rectum had been, allowing Albert to catch a close glimpse of her moist ocean flower and his breath. She covered his nose and mouth, again smothering him, this time while taking his member in her mouth. Visions of Bronson and the associated memories of Richard prompted her to suck him off. She licked the engorged head, laving it completely until it glistened in the light.

She moved down the shaft in a straight line, to his balls— her teeth gripped his left cherry and squeezed it just hard enough for a painful thrill, then released it with a smacking sound. She went back to the head, lashing it again, flicking the tip, teasing it where it joined the shaft. A quick look up, a smug smile, and she plunged down and engulfed him with her mouth, now intent on making him spurt. She clasped his prick with her lips, reveling in the way she could feel him expanding in response to her attentions. He came in an infinitely pleasurable way . . . in what seemed like an instant away from suffocating.

# CHAPTER 7

It rained for days—heavy, unseasonably warm rain that brought Berliners to their balconies for the air. Water washed the streets, but the city could never lose it grimy quality, Jan thought. When the storms died down, the drizzle looked like coal dust as it fell from the patchy gray sky. Amid other pedestrians in the late afternoon, Jan walked home after work—down Warschauerstrasse toward Boxhagenerstrasse, eyeing the buildings still riddled with bullet holes from the war.

What am I, a Pole—the French of the Slavs—doing in exile in Germany? He habitually took stock even though he knew this circumspection was antithetical to his conception of reality: space and time filled with acts, not thoughts, unless he included the act of thinking. Acts like cleaning drizzle from his glasses on his shirt sleeve conditioned his intuitive perception of reality, the chain of cause and effect. The sidewalk's effect was to make me a pedestrian, he thought, yet the same sidewalk serves dogs as a toilet. A bald woman with a bouquet of flowers in her basket pedaled by on an old bike, smiling at a little dog playing with a bright yellow ball near a portal wall. Reality—actuality, as he sometimes called it—was relative. As a writer, the clerk saw the relationship of all things as being framed by the ever-changing chronos and topos: the chronotope, as the Russian philosopher Bakhtin, who was also born in what was once Poland, put it.

He'd had a few shots of vodka with the boys in the kitchen after work, so the feminine movements and flashes of color instantly caught his eye—two young women emerged from a laundromat carrying a bag of clothes between them. The rain seemed to stop and a ray of sun pierced the clouds. He noticed how they turned in tandem, how the black woman's dark nipples protruded through her orange bodysuit like the extruded letters on a billboard. He noticed the bare midriff of the white woman, who glanced sideways at her friend, then over her shoulder at the clerk.

The clerk spied the seam of the white woman's jeans digging into her meaty pussy, the ripple of delicate muscles on the black woman's back, then back to the white woman's naked spine. The heavy bag of clothes swayed between them like a kid's game. A rare, warm day in fall. Now or never, the clerk thought, or better said, here and now. The women turned the corner—Jan hurried to them.

"Can I come?" he asked the white woman.

It took her a moment to respond, as if she hadn't fully understood the question. Had he been in Warsaw, he would have been much more romantic, more polite. Perhaps he would have said, "Excuse me, miss, may I speak with you for a moment? I apologize for interrupting you, but it's hard not to notice how beautiful you are. Allow me to introduce myself." If she had extended her hand, he would have kissed it.

"I don't know," she said in abject German, "can you?"

"Come where?" the black woman wanted to know in slightly better German.

"Wherever you're going," he said in English.

"We're going straight to Hell," the black woman said, adding, "you can come if you want."

"Very generous of you. From the looks of your laundry, you've been in Berlin some time now."

"We love it," the white woman said.

"Oh, you do? I would imagine that American women couldn't get along without your conveniences—the smooth roads, the dishwashers that keep your hands smooth."

The black woman laughed. "Wait till you see where we live."

They crossed Kreutzigerstrasse at the park where young women picked blossoms from their apples and jugglers practiced with oranges, wooden pins and hats. The clerk stepped aside for a passing baby carriage.

"Are you a Berliner?" the white woman said.

He shook his head. "What gave you that idea?"

"Your German . . . it sounded like . . ."

"A Berliner," he finished her phrase for her and answered her next question without being asked: "No, I'm from Warsaw. Things are desperate there. I was on my way to Paris, but this is as far as I could go."

"We went to Warsaw, remember?" the white woman asked her friend.

They passed storefronts on one side and parked cars on the other.

"Yeah, I remember," the black woman said. "We'd heard all about Polish men being the most handsome and romantic men in Europe. We found our handsome men, but all they wanted to do was exchange money."

"Ha, that doesn't surprise me. As for the reputation of Polish men, well, I could tell you a few jokes that might dispel any misconceptions you have."

"So this is Hell," the white woman said.

The clerk took in the graffiti-blasted squat: KILL THE COPS, LOOTING IS NOT A CRIME, AMBITION IS SUBMISSION. The double-locked door opened onto a demolished foyer. They moved into the candlelight emanating from a makeshift alcove to the right that smelled like a crack den. In the shadows, a guy mindlessly toyed with a knife.

"Before we put on the locks," the white woman began, "worse drunks than you would wander in here, sleep a few hours, and wander out."

They stepped into a dark hall, the women turning sideways with their laundry. Weak daylight cast through a freshly mounted window onto still more unfinished wood on the repair-spotted staircase. Steps cast faint, saw-tooth shadows on the wall. Halfway up the first flight—the black woman in the lead—his eyes narrowed on the swaying black ass and ivory belly.

"Let me help you with that." He slung the duffel bag over his shoulder and followed them up more flights of rickety stairs.

"A gentleman—we don't get that much around here, do we?" the black woman said.

"No, unfortunately. Maybe we could get him to help with the water." The white woman unlocked a door made of gnarled concrete reinforcement rods.

The black woman moved inside while the white woman held the door open. He hauled the laundry into a series of interconnecting, partially open rooms—scuffed floors, a wood stove and smokestack hammered into place, obscene paintings on blown-out walls. Partitions held curtains half-obscuring evidence of the many people who lived there. The bag spilled open on the center table—the lingerie forced the clerk to strain to maintain an indifferent expression.

"It's hard to keep clean without water," the white woman said.

"Yeah, I would imagine," the clerk murmured.

The door to the fridge was open, disclosing putrid vegetables in the crannies. Dirty diapers were piled on the closet floor. A cross-eyed woman peeked around a partition, her pregnant belly bulging into view. A cross-eyed kid held her leg. Toys, wire—spools of it uncovered for sale as scrap—tools and tampons lay scattered on the irreparable floor. A candle burned next to a Buddhist shrine, dangerously close to a spacey drawing. High breasts rubbed against the clerk's elbow. He pulled his hand out of his pocket and shot a sideways glance to see whose tits they were—a short, strong woman with close-cropped hair. He cleaned his glasses on his shirt, not sure if he could trust his eyes.

A tall skinny guy with his hand in a cast from a fight with a wall followed the short woman into the room, the neck of a bottle held loosely in his fingers.

"Did you paint that on?" the guy asked the black woman as he scratched her close-cropped head.

"Oh, no—he's got a bottle," she said, ignoring his remark. "Hey, Natasha, let us know when to call the cops. It's a good thing you traded beds with the guy downstairs so we don't have to hear you two fuck."

"Don't worry, you'll still hear us," the guy said, slipping behind a screen.

The walls shook as someone in the building banged on the pipes. Muffled curses came from behind the screens. The clerk put his Brecht glasses back on and ran his hand through his spiky blond hair. The pounding reverberated through the walls, stopped for a moment, started again. The white woman caught him staring.

"Would you help us shower? We usually go to the Relax Center, but it's so expensive."

He nodded.

They took him up another flight and nimbly led him along catwalks, loose planks running over the rafters. Empty buckets and ropes on a plywood sheet. The white woman looked down on a bathtub on the lower floor.

"We'll fill up these buckets at the hydrant on the street so you can pull the buckets up with the rope." The black woman pointed out a hole hammered through the facade. "When we get back inside, just pour the water through the hole in the floor so we can wash up."

"Small job," he said.

The clerk looked out the hole at the surrounding squats, including one emblazoned THE ALTER NATIVE, and the gray rooftops of Berlin. Cars rumbled over the cobblestone street below. To the right, construction was underway in the changing neighborhood. Church bells rang and the smoldering cold sun descended in the western sky.

Four female hands—two black, two white—on a pipe wrench attached to a hydrant. He ducked into the musty room, and scrambling over planks, gathered the heavy rope in coils. He lowered the giant bucket out the hole with a grunt and watched as the women pulled on the wrench, his glasses slipping down his nose. He carefully folded them in a handkerchief and stuck them in a crevice in the stone wall.

"What are you waiting for? Heave ho!" the black woman called from the street.

I'd like a cigarette to enjoy this fuzzy view, he thought, but I smoke too much anyway. He rolled up the sleeves to his heavily starched, white shirt, one of two he owned. From that height—without his glasses—the women were stick figures, the water gushing into a bucket, a drip from a faucet.

The illusion of my faulty senses, he thought as he pulled the rope hand-over-hand, spilling water on the side of the building. He wasn't so critical of his senses that he made reality conform to concepts; he arrived at conclusions that were often in turn refuted by experience. The absence of clear vision heightened his other senses and forced him to constantly reconcile his thoughts with his actions.

I'll need a shower too, he thought, before this is over. Sweet-smelling sweat, like freshly baked bread, formed on his brow and his face reddened into what might be mistaken as a healthy glow—actually an alcoholic flush. He lifted the bucket through the hole in the wall. His arms were sore, he tore off his shirt.

"I'll need a drink before this is over," he said to the women, now in the bathroom below, as they undressed each other. The clerk sat on a plank, dangling his legs through the hole to the lower floor. He heard them giggle, but he didn't look until one tugged on his leather shoe. Between his legs, he saw two of the most lovely women he'd seen since his university days. My glasses, he remembered.

"Quit gawking."

"I can hardly see a thing in this light," he said.

Emergency candles began to burn in soap dishes over the sink, giving the white tiles a mustard hue. He doused the women with water and watched their luscious skin turn to lather—the mesmerizing sight of flesh coruscating with soap bubbles in candlelight. The white woman washed the black's back, then called up for more water. The clerk dumped another bit, then caught the white woman by surprise.

She smiled up at him through strands of wet hair as he took off his shoes, trousers and shorts. He stood over the hole.

"Take a look at that," she said.

Just as she tilted her head up, he caught her with a splash.

"No fair," she said. "I wasn't ready."

"You were looking up here," he said, looking at them past his half-hard cock. "Get ready—here comes the last of it."

He poured and before they could dry off, before the goosebumps subsided, he eased through the hole in the floor and tumbled on the wet tiles, laughing. The women fell on him—the black woman licked his cock as the white woman straddled his head. Water dripped from her pussy onto his face.

The Gates of Hell, he mused—thoughts reverberated around his skull like the pipes in the walls—only better than Rodin, more akin to heaven. His barrel chest heaved as he gasped for air, his back slipped slightly on the tile floor. They grow fine women in America, he reflected, too bad they're such Philistines. I'll never get to Paris at this rate—giving my love away, to Americans no less. What I'd give for a French woman with a fine sense of aesthetics and superb intelligence. Where else would I find my *ultraphilosophe*? Perhaps Russia—go there like Balzac to find a woman with whom I can speak soul to soul, as they say in Moscow.

While these thoughts danced though his mind, he serviced the two young American women by instinct. The light touch of his tongue over an erect clitoris framed by pretty blond hairs while full lips sucked him. He eased his fingers to her face and brushed her smooth dark skin in such beautiful contrast to the wet blond pussy waving before his blurry eyes. Big black lips in hand now, his thumb over her upper lip and index finger under her lower lip forming a blissful seal, he pumped as the hot blonde slit above him settled on his mouth.

In this position, they could easily suffocate him—and he might not know what was happening until it was too late. Black lip pressure, so full and soft, up and down on his member as he bucked into her. His hand left the lips, he raised it and the other hand, still holding his breath, onto the white bottom and raised the tender pink flesh off his face. With pantherish movements he moved behind the other and kneaded her luscious black buns, the flesh seeping between his fingers and beyond his hand as he dug into her deeply.

The black woman rose on her knees, and to his surprise, kept coming. She pushed him over on his butt, sinking onto his cock, straddling him backwards, waving the great black smudges of her buns and even darker line between them before his weak eyes as she descended. She grabbed him harder with his pussy, made an adjustment, and fully impaled herself on him. Gasps flooded his ears as his cock surged in and oozed over moist tissue, pushing it apart, snaking into her. Her head hung forward, out of sight. Muscles rippling down her slender back. He felt her lower back tense as she raised herself. The high, jutting arcs of flesh smoothly slid into his hands. He squeezed her hotly, sucking in his breath.

The white woman sucked her friend's tits with big smacking sounds, while the clerk simply watched black ass move as it had on the street, with a sweeping, swaying motion of her hips, pulling him with her wetness and sinking into him. Screams came from the big-chested tart being mercilessly fucked by the drunk with the broken hand.

"Someone should call the cops."

The clerk couldn't tell which one said it.

"He'll probably fuck her to death one of these days."

"I'm tempted to buy him a bottle and give him a go myself."

"Maybe . . . I don't know."

Angry thoughts filled the clerk's brain. They treat me as if I'm a rack of meat. Maybe that's what they want; they want to be fucked to death. Let me at the cunt who begs for such abuse. I'll give them what they want.

In movements that dissimulated his fury—movements that nonetheless seemed to signify that he had received their call to action—the clerk calmly pushed himself off the floor, and with his cock still in place, he prodded the woman toward the tub. Before she could grasp the side, he fucked her over it with forceful strokes until her belly was draped over the smooth, porcelain edge. He pulled the white woman onto her friend's back. She came willingly, if questioningly.

He manipulated her legs, like so much clay, into position. With one woman on top of the other, he pulled out of the black woman and immediately plunged into her friend. He drove into the yielding flesh, stabbing her time and time again. Alternating endlessly . . . black and white . . . white and black . . . the latter finally screaming like the big-titted woman downstairs. A candle burned out with a flickering light in the broken mirror and the white woman melted on the floor like wax.

He filled the holy space between the black woman's legs with his white come. The second flame drowned in a pool of wax, and with each moment the room grew darker—the dimming, crepuscular rays of the vanished sun as it filtered through the glazed bathroom window. He felt as if he were being sucked into a black hole.

The black woman smiled at him from the shadows. "Hey," she said softly, "what's your name?"

"Grabawhiski."

"Ha, ha, Grab-a-whiski—I get it. We'll find you a drink, but you got any more Polish jokes?"

"You got a hanger so I can get my girlfriend out of my car?"

# CHAPTER 8

Richard turned back the lapel of his green nylon jacket, revealing the seal-and-snake insignia of his water polo club. The clerk behind the security station of the Sport and Relax Center on Leninallee rolled his eyes for Richard to enter. The audacity of wearing anything Stasi, now, he thought, but the clerk nonetheless pressed the button under his console. Richard pushed his massive body through the turnstile without inserting a token.

The ultramodern sports complex, at this school hour, was near empty. He surveyed the volleyball and basketball courts, the café, billiard table, weight room and interconnecting pools. Richard took justifiable pride in the way his socialist state provided for its youth. With the indoor ice rink next door, he asked himself, where would you find another place like this? Nowhere in West Berlin. He stepped into the locker room.

"We thought you were already in the water," Hans said.

Richard nodded. "Soon enough."

"We thought you might want to burn off some of the fat you've put on since you started working at the bakery," Gerrit said.

"I'd rather bake bread than shred paper," Richard began, adding: "Get out as soon as you can—but covering your tracks probably won't help. You're more likely to be jailed for a cover-up than anything you did while Honecker was in power."

Gerrit shook his head. "You sound like you're ready to follow your wife and kids to the west."

"I would if she would have me." Richard lowered his head. "She'll never forgive me for Adina. I let myself get carried away with that young one."

"From the looks of it, a westie—some filmmaker—has her now," Hans said.

Albert belonged to a small video exchange club. Richard's Stasi contacts in the west had investigated Adina for him and come up with the tape. The team had seen it.

"Adina looks good in a swim cap. I wonder what made her want to wear it?"

"Or the lipstick on her cunt." They laughed.

"Maybe it was for you, Richard," Gerrit teased.

"No, if Adina used lipstick anywhere for Richard, it was on her tits. 'Suck these,' she used to beg, remember?" the goalie said.

"How could I forget," Hans added. "Did you see her blowing kisses to the camera? I thought they were for me."

"You want to kick a guy when he's down?" Richard said. "Go ahead. Why don't you mention the bald spot that's growing on the back of my head or that my cock is shrinking." He slammed his locker shut, the sound produced silence. "If you ask me, you don't have bragging rights after the way Spandau kicked our butts."

"Shit," Hans replied. "They are one of the best polo teams in Europe. So what if we lost one match?"

"So, I was the only one to score a goal," Richard said. "See you in the water."

"You know what I think?" the goalie asked the two-meter man as Richard left the room. "I think losing the apartment pissed him off more than anything."

"Yeah, I heard he's pimping on the side now. The apartment would've helped him in his new profession."

Richard stepped into the pool area. He was drawn to a young woman emerging from the pool like a golden vision of perfection—she slid, climbed, crawled and stroked her way down to the other pools via cascading waterfalls and swirling eddies. Her unlined, white bikini was transparent, hardly veiling her rose-colored nipples and light fur.

Richard, meanwhile, whirled his massive arms, warming up for the full scrimmage in a few moments. She looked the other way as if to say, I don't see you, but there was no way she could miss the aquajock with his cap including ear guards. At ten meters she had trouble guessing his age.

Let's see if he's interested, the blond said to herself as she became encircled in the pond at the base of the waterfall by young mothers and their babies. Getting out of the pond, she allowed the string bikini to slip down her buns. Golden moss protruded from the front of her suit and half her crack was exposed as she walked to the diving well.

She retied her strings, climbed the ladder and faced Richard atop the ten-meter board. Although she wasn't as tall as Adina, Richard noted she was more muscular and athletic. He was surprised by her bravado and stopped warming up to see what she would do. Feet together, arms lowered to her sides, eyes on the steel catapult, she took three sure strides and leapt up, came down on the board, flew up in the air.

She executed a controlled swan dive with half a twist, leaving a respectably small splash. The impact stripped her bare. Richard saw nothing of her until she surfaced at the end of the diving well, bobbing out the sides of her top, and then lifting herself out of the water in one smooth motion with her bottoms around her thighs. She regrouped in front of him as though it was nothing unusual.

"Looks like you have a new admirer," Hans said to Richard as he, and a few others, joined the old man on the deck.

"I'm the one admiring her," Richard answered, loud enough for her to hear.

"Did we come here to practice or do some women-watching?" the goalie asked.

Gerrit threw the dimpled ball in the Olympic-size polo court and knifed in after it.

They couldn't care less about me, the blond thought as she watched the muscular men go through their drills: 100-meter, 50-meter sprints; 25 meters heads up; the same distance underwater. As the team did 200-meter sprints with momentary rests at the 50 mark, she noticed Richard look up to see if she was watching. She strutted over to the canal that led to a rubber flap and waded under it to an outdoor pool.

"I'll show these young punks," Richard said to himself.

He was the last line of defense before the goalie. The two-meter man swam straight to a wet pass, came to a quick stop, and kicked to get off a shot. Richard stayed with him—he half-sunk his opponent with one hand and blocked the shot with the other. The batted ball skidded away. The two-meter man grabbed Richard's treelike leg; Richard kicked him and came after him. They fought for a moment, an intense underwater moment—eyes open, straining to see through silver bubbles. Richard grabbed the two-meter man by the throat with one fist and the guy's arm with the other—arm straining against arm—and then punched him in the nose. The old man broke free, dove with the ball and surfaced in open water.

The batted ball in his control, Richard arched his back, crawled with his head up, changing directions through the defense. He made a blind pass to himself off the back of a defender's head. Laughing at them, he rolled out to the right, working off a screen, splashing defenders. Suddenly he rose up with eggbeater kicks and slung a left-handed sweep shot by the goalie. That'll teach them, Richard thought as he swam back to his position at the other end of the pool.

\*

On his way out of practice, Richard noticed the exquisite blond diver. She was watching a badminton game from the balcony above the courts, her head slowly following the birdie from side to side.

"Do you come here often?" Richard wrapped his hands around the rail. "I've never seen you here before." He peered into her blue eyes. "If I had, I would have remembered."

"Oh, I used to come here often as a teenager. I just lost my job . . ." The thought momentarily silenced her. "So many of us have, now that former GDR citizens shop in the west and our factories have been privatized." She pronounced the last word with disdain. Raising her voice, she added, "Which is another way of saying *closed*."

"The situation is awful," Richard said.

"So I've started coming back here to pass the time. It's too depressing to stay home all day with the rats. Two of those monsters were in the communal toilet this morning when I went to pee."

"Yes, the housing situation . . ." His thoughts drifted off. "I used to think that the authorities should demolish all the old buildings, then it occurred to me, we would have nowhere to live."

"Life's full of traps," was all she could think of to say at first, then, in a soft voice, as if speaking to herself, "Just not the ones I need . . . you know, the rat traps."

"I'm meeting a few people at the Alex. Want to come along?"

"If I leave the center, I won't be able to get back in. I don't want to go home to the rats."

"I'll only be with these people a few minutes." Richard grinned down at her from his towering height. "After my meeting, we can go out to eat. My treat."

"I would like that."

Richard ushered her outside into the grim street at dusk. They climbed onto a waiting tram. Children filled the aisle and the front seats were taken. Richard led her past the noisy kids to a seat in the back. The wooden floor slats creaked and then cracked as his weight pressed on them. People looked up for a second, then away when they saw his intimidating presence. Even with the prospect of a new young lover, Richard thought, even with this youthful manifestation of life, nothing could obscure the reality of a social system in decay. This is no way to live. The gray sky weighed heavily, as he saw it, on the uncertain future.

The tram dropped them at the Alex. Richard led her across a corner of the large brick square and checked the world time clock outside the Berliner Kaffeehaus. He was late.

"Promise me that you won't make a scene regardless of what's discussed," Richard said.

"Why would I do that?" she asked.

"These are dangerous times," Richard commented, then hastened to add as he held the door for her, "What's your name?"

"Anya."

Richard stepped inside behind her, wrapped his arm around her back and whispered: "All right Anya, don't worry about anything as long as you're with me—Richard."

A host approached them, but Richard dismissed him with a wave and directed Anya down an aisle with the upscale, open kitchen on one side and tables on the other. At first glance, Anya thought the men sitting along the back wall were soldiers because their hair was so short—nearly shaved. But their clothing—rolled up sleeves, suspenders—and their markings—tattoos, scars—told her they were working class delinquents who had wandered to the far right.

Most of the Stasi were worried about the fate of their nearly six thousand nonofficial collaborators in the west and did everything possible to conceal their identities. Despite Richard's anti-fascist roots, he and a few of his colleagues were preoccupied with using eastern skinheads against feminists and other protesters, despite the risk of losing control of their mercenaries. As Richard and Anya approached the table, two skins discussed their favorite band, Final Solution, and the other skin was reading something in *New Order*—probably something, Richard thought, written by a revisionist in Nebraska where such thinking was not outlawed.

"Oi."

Richard looked at their blank faces. "Right. What have you been doing lately?"

"We've been quite busy, actually." The skin spoke over the top of his paper. "Lots of recruits coming from Saxony, Westphalia."

The waiter arrived. Richard ordered beers for everyone except himself; he had tea.

"I hope you're telling these new recruits something constructive."

"Absolutely."

"Something besides racism. I don't like immigrants either, but you're giving us Germans a bad name again."

The waiter came with a tray of drinks, leaving a little receipt in front of Richard. Anya studied Richard and the boys over the gold rim of her glass as she sipped the pilsner.

"I'm surprised you wanted to meet here," Richard said as he pulled the teabag out of his cup.

"The Alex is ours," the lanky skin said. He made an emphatic gesture toward the window with a hand wrapped in leather strips. "And it always will be."

Richard just laughed, thinking that eventually he would run them off to the west as his grandfather had done to the SS.

The burly skin with a clean-shaven, roundish head looked at the one with the newspaper. "Can we tell him?"

"Since Richard no longer functions in any official capacity, I don't see any harm. Is she reliable?"

Richard nodded.

"Oi." The burly skin uttered the porcine sound that had migrated from Britain in right-wing circles. "Seventy attacks in two days. What do you think of that?" Before Richard could answer, the skin elaborated: "We threw a guy from Mozambique out of a streetcar and trashed a Vietnamese shop."

"Yeah, we even pushed a Red Army soldier preparing to leave Germany out of a third story window and stole his rifle."

"I like that last one," Richard said.

The lanky skin rested his leather-strapped hand on the table, rattling the glasses slightly. "More weapons are arriving daily from Austria," he said.

"Well, it sounds like you're ready for the Autonomes," Richard said calmly, referring to the squatters who had occupied numerous buildings near the communal bachelor pad.

"Oi."

As Richard sipped his weak tea, the skins passed a small bottle of korn[21] under the table, taking sips, chasing them with beer.

"Very good, comrades. I'll let you know when and where. Some of my people should be able to help. We'll certainly have materiel for you."

Richard nodded to Anya and began to get up.

"Do you think you could at least help with the bill?" the leader asked.

"Forgive me, I almost forgot." Richard put numerous bills on the table. "Enjoy yourselves."

Richard led Anya outside the café. "Things must be really bad if criminals have to beg. It's as if there is nothing left to steal."

"Why do you deal with them, then? What's going on?"

"Never mind. Let's eat at a little bar I know. It's not too far from here. We can walk."

They started walking on Liebknechtstrasse as dusk descended.

"Where do you live?"

Anya pointed ahead. "Just off Prenzlauer."

---

21     A distilled spirit made from rye.

She meant the working class tenements that were becoming overrun with dropouts—musicians, painters, aging hippies, punks—as well as yuppies who found the older apartments, with their high ceilings and ornate moulding, charming.

"That's a lousy neighborhood. I should be back in a nice flat next week," Richard said.

They walked arm in arm, left on Memhard, which he knew from his training, then turned into Munz, which turned into Gips. Richard couldn't help thinking about Adina in the west. He had taught her everything and then she just went away, as had his wife. Anya, he remembered, was roughly the same age as his daughter.

"Where did you work?" Richard asked as they turned right on the narrow, diagonal side street.

"I was a secretary for the head of the city's dairy distribution works. It was a very good job and I was close to my boss. He took me with him on business trips to the processing plants. You know what I mean?"

"No."

"I was more than just his secretary. When he got the ax, so did I."

"I understand. Where is he now?"

"He went back to his wife—there was nothing I could do." Richard suddenly stopped in front of a pharmacy. "Wait here."

He left her standing on the street like a stray cat. Why shouldn't I go in with him? She wondered. Is he sick? She was somewhat reassured as Richard emerged with a package that was too large to be pills.

"Can I put this in your purse?"

"What is it?"

"I'll tell you later."

Richard stuffed the package in her purse and kissed the golden locks on her forehead. Left on Pieck. Around the corner they spotted an aging woman with a pay phone to her ear—she leaned out of the booth and began shouting at a young man as he walked away, headed toward the couple.

"I have to make a call by five." The man llooked at Richard helplessly. "She's been on the line for twenty minutes."

"Say, lady," Richard chimed in, "can't you make it quick? These are public phones."

She hung up without saying anything to whomever, if anyone, was on the other end. An ancient bicycle leaned on the booth—she mounted it, and as she pedaled off, she saluted the three of them. Nazis, Richard thought, they're still everywhere.

"Thank you," the young man said. "I didn't want any trouble."

"She must be senile," Anya said.

The couple again walked arm in arm, now crossing paths with industrial workers heading home on the cobblestone street. Smokestacks rose across the western sky as a wino lay on the sidewalk, passed out next to a public urinal, hugging himself as he slept. Darkness had fallen on the cool Berlin air like the inside of a chilled, hard-boiled egg. Silence broken by delinquent boys who ran away from the sex workers, heckling each other under the streetlamps at Oranienburger Tor.

The Free Ring, with its boxing gloves sign, loomed before them. There were four steps up to the door—Anya moved up first, Richard held her by her waist. Two workers in overalls stumbled came out the door and stumbled down the steps—one with a beer in hand, a big guy.

Richard stepped out of his way. "Watch where you're going."

"Fuck off."

Richard opened the door for Anya and she stepped in, moving past an older sex worker wearing an eye patch. The sight startled Anya, whose eyes darted around the room at the rough-looking people.

"What is this place?"

"Just a neighborhood restaurant. Fine with you?"

"Yes, I just . . . was curious."

Low lights and lusterless wood walls. They took a seat at a wooden table toward the back. A waitress cleared a nearby table and glanced in Richard's direction.

"What would you like?"

"I'll have a pork knuckle sandwich. How about you Anya? Some fried Camembert?"

She nodded.

"And two pilsners."

Anya gazed at the stern face of the woman seated across the restaurant, at the head of a long table, she almost looked male, if not for her pretty breasts that swayed freely under her tee shirt. She was with a guy with a broken arm in a sling and another with a small bandage over his bruised eye. Anya could hear they spoke 'real' German, trading insults and laughter during the course of their conversation.

With a look of indifference, a sex worker wearing a butt thong over sheer stockings came in from the cold. As soon as she stepped inside, a brute in a suit spun her once in an impromptu jig; she gave him a peck on his stubbly cheek and a gentle shove out the door. Her figure—showcasing a high ass—moved toward the back of the bar, stopped at Richard's table.

"So, Richard, breaking in a new woman?"

"None of your business. I'm just showing Anya the terrain." He turned to his dinner companion. "Anya, this is Charlotte."

The women exchanged glances just as beer and food arrived. Plates and mugs rattled on the table, the bartender hurried back behind his bar.

"Anya is unemployed." Richard took a bite of his pork knuckle sandwich. "I thought I'd be a sport and buy her a meal. Care to join us?"

"No, but I'll tell you this, sweetie," Charlotte said to Anya. "There's no reason not to have a job when cocks are as hard as the times." Charlotte turned to Richard. "I'll be with the other women if you need me." She started toward the back room, then turned back. "Weren't you going to get something for us?"

"Let me finish eating."

Charlotte nodded, glanced back at Anya and wandered off. Richard raised his glass to Anya. "Here's to knowing how to live."

Anya had a bite of fried Camembert in her mouth. She raised her glass and washed down the cheese with beer. Richard's chair creaked as he leaned back to swallow. Their neighbor at the next table—a well-dressed gent with a cigar between his teeth—slumped forward, resting his elbows on his table and his head in his hand. A dog wandered into the bar, and the chef stuck his head out of the kitchen door, calling to the dog. A burly worker with a small mustache and a Greek sailor's cap petted the dog; nose in the air, she trotted away, smelling something good in the kitchen.

"Do you like me just a little bit?" Richard asked, tickling Anya under the chin with his brawny finger.

"Yes, I like you a little bit."

"With me, you can live well on love."

Anya put down her fork. "What are you saying?"

"I'm saying that I am the man of this house. Anyone who wants to run the Free Ring has to fight me. I'd crush them like ants."

Richard feigned smashing the table with his savage hand, then reached to Anya's face and gave her a caress.

"I'm not sure."

"I provide my young women with security in the place they choose to eat and drink—here and their hotel is next door. It's very comfortable."

"I could stay there?"

"With the money I give you tonight, yes. Tomorrow you'd have to find customers, but you're fresh, so that shouldn't be a problem."

"What about AIDS?"

"May I?" Richard reached for her purse and took out his package. "Never do anything without one of these." He opened the package and took out a condom. "You know how this works, don't you?"

"Yeah, sure."

"Let's find out."

"Where?"

"There's a little room back there."

He stepped over to the bar and overheard the bartender tell a patron speaking of brotherly love to shut up. Richard reached over the counter and grabbed a RESERVED sign.

"Hey, I need that for a table," the bartender barked as he filled mugs with beer.

"Don't give me your petty merchant's logic," Richard said. "Besides, I probably won't last long."

Richard returned to the table and set the sign amid their unfinished meal. With his powerful fingers he partially eased Anya's blouse off her smooth white shoulder. The gent in the suit looked up from his cigar—her push-up bra and the glints of light reflecting off Anya's earring and Richard's steel wristwatch caught his bloodshot eye.

Richard led Anya—who snatched up her purse—by the hand through the smoky bar. Several sex workers occupied a large table in an adjacent room. Their clients weren't coming so they drank and ate and played cards. Big hair and G-strings, Anya noted, was the common uniform.

"Why don't you tell that one-eyed cunt that Poland is only forty miles away," one whore said to Richard in a Rhineland accent.

"I'm sure she knows she's closer to home than you," Richard said as they walked by.

"You can't go in there," Charlotte said.

Richard gripped a doorknob. "Why?"

"It's occupied."

"I'm occupied territory. You'll have to wait your turn," a soprano sang from the other side of the door.

"Ungh, ungh," Charlotte grunted, adding loud enough for the John to hear, "Don't forget to take off your hat."

Richard steered Anya by the waist toward the bathroom. By now he had reconciled himself to the fact that he couldn't unite his spiritual and sensual feeling around the same woman. He was more inclined to take his love wherever it presented itself. Fucking Anya in the bathroom of the Free Ring would serve as a fine initiation to her newly chosen profession. Anya had tried and failed to find work so many times she felt as though she had little choice, and in other ways, she had made love for money before.

LAW IS THE VASELINE USED TO FUCK WORKERS UP THE ASS was scrawled in lipstick across the tiles on the bathroom wall.

"Who the hell?" Richard shook his head at the graffiti and guided her into the stall—bent her over the tank. "At least there's no rats in the toilet."

She closed the seat cover. "I've never done anything like this. What if someone comes in?"

"They won't. Not if I'm in here. Not if they know what's good for them."

Richard eased off her right shoe, then took off one leg of her jeans and panties.

"You have nothing to fear," he whispered in her ear.

Why did he say that? She felt his weight on her back. He might kill me with that thing. It felt big to her as it traveled over the underside of her ass and nosed out from her loins like the cock of a normal man. Half his length rubbed against her—the rest was in her hand. For an instant, Anya felt like a young man jerking off over the toilet, but the sensation was overtaken by a genuinely feminine desire born from contact with his smooth flesh. He massaged her ass-cheeks with his hands; and with his thrusts between her legs, he mashed against her moistness.

Anya reached for the condoms in her purse, spilling the open box in her excitement. They scattered across the bathroom floor. Richard let out a low laugh. What is he laughing about? She wondered. He was the one who told me not to do anything without a condom. She tore open the foil package and tried to roll the rubber over the mushroom head of his cock.

"Don't waste your time. It probably won't go on and if it does, it'll break," Richard said.

"But you said . . ."

"It's different with me. I'm the man of the house."

Richard aimed at her succulent slit, at the wrinkled wet flesh that stretched smooth as he surged in halfway. She's tight, but not too much, he thought, convinced she'd been with sportsmen before. He pulled her toward him, sinking deeper into the eternal female abyss as Anya let out a little scream.

Hoots from the bar filtered into the bathroom.

"Ssshhh," Richard hissed, "you want them to think you're a pro."

She edged forward with his thrusts, as if trying to escape. Her face pressed sideways against the wall and she groaned softly. He established a tawdry rhythm—in and out just a bit while going round and round. Anya held the tank and gritted her teeth as he forced her hips back with his hands. Her neck hurt so she reached up and pushed herself off the wall with one hand. and gripped the tank tighter with the other. He oozed in deeper from behind, searching for the bottom of her vagina, finding it and backing off a little, then grinding in plunging circles.

He marveled at her filmy skin and lightly muscled back that tensed responsively. The slight creases where she was fleshy drew him in. He snapped her bra and ran his hands under her torso, searching for the pink nipples he'd seen at the pool. His movements grew faster as he found them. She gasped as he hunched over her and pulled them together. He was losing control of his terrible, vein-bulging body—furrowed face, open mouth, half-shut eyes, stretched neck, quivering legs. Little shrieks of pain issued from her lips, which only spurred him on. His other hand moved down her slim ribs to her belly, grabbing and releasing the taut flesh, his nose buried in tufts of chlorine-scented hair.

Fresh pussy at long last, he thought. It thrilled him to again open a vagina to full womanhood, as he had done with Adina. He gripped her hips and brushed her cervix with each spasm. Then he drew back and admired his cock as it made her pussy stretch smooth. If she could see me now, he thought of Adina as he took in the veined topography of his member and her moist hairs. He plunged in again with a sneer on his dry lips. This was how he liked them—young, tight, willing to do whatever he demanded. He fucked her roughly, his balls slapping her thighs, his sweaty belly making sucking noises each time it collided with, and pulled away from, her little ass.

He felt huge, even more colossal than usual, because she was small, and he got smug satisfaction knowing it felt at least somewhat painful for her. Renewed strokes with his thighs twining into knots from powerful thrusts, he exploded in her and continued erupting and thrusting. The excess dripped down her thighs. She eased down and her legs straddled the toilet bowl; her head fell against her arms, which were crossed on top of the tank. She felt faint. Richard leaned against the stall door. Sweat streamed down his forehead. Suddenly the door opened: Charlotte and Patricia.

"These days, a whore is born every day," Charlotte said, sizing up Anya's naked ass and dripping cunt.

Patricia looked past Richard's flaccid member at the condoms. "So you did remember."

The two pros fell to their knees and gathered up the packets.

# CHAPTER 9

As usual, Albert was asleep. He had taken a tranquilizer immediately after Adina did it to him, buying himself a trip to never-never land on his Persian carpet. The pill bottle and a half-empty glass of water stood on the coffee table. He still wasn't allowed in his own room, now the forbidden room, without Adina's permission. She looked at him from the door. What does he dream of, Adina wondered to herself as she watched him sleep, bigger and bigger whips?

Sleep, perverted sex, videos—Albert didn't seem to want anything he couldn't buy, which made sense to Adina in a matter-of-fact way, as he was quite wealthy. She paced the apartment like a caged animal with a vague sense of dissatisfaction, then she mindlessly made herself a cup of sweet tea, unsuccessfully trying to sound reveille with the kettle.

She brought the cup over to the window. Rain pattered against the pane, and she felt the bittersweet pain of wanting what couldn't be bought, the intangible belonging she had in the east with Richard, with the women at work and her parents being closer. How many Sundays will I spend like this? She slowly stirred her tea, feeling lonely and bored, and put the spoon on the sill.

Her reflection in the window formed a screen to that part of her inner being consigned to others as her form was superimposed on an empty, rain-beaten cityscape. There were no others now, only Albert, covered by a wool blanket except for his childish, sleep-swollen face. In the east, it was different. Even though her mother was the newly elected mayor of the village, she would be home on Sunday. Her dog and cat were there, and the friendly woods she knew so well. Adina had explained this to Albert and he promised that Sunday would be their day together. Yet it was also the day to clean the apartment and to get ready for the work week. If he did go out, it was to play tennis, which she liked because she wore short tennis dresses to show off her legs and sometimes more to his partners.

Adina looked away from the somber, wet streets that reminded her of the cold gesellschaft[22] relations among people in the west and the legal contract between her and Albert. She stared at him sleeping on the carpet, totally indifferent to her, indifferent to everything that was life, like a character in those films by Wim Wenders he likes so much. Albert's primary exception was work and, like her father, he seemed to love it passionately. Is that life? She turned and looked at him. What good is his work to me? Sure, he makes good money, but he's not making a film about me and wouldn't even take me to a cinema because he has to concentrate at every showing. Film was the one subject he could teach me the most about, she thought, but he never took the time. And with his constant search for images, his every waking moment was work. He once said he even works in his sleep.

---

[22]   Society and the sociology category representing indirect relations and impersonal roles.

Once he had taken her to the opera. She loved it—not so much the music but being part of the well-dressed bourgeois crowd. Unfortunately, he made this date only after a fight about seeing films. Films, films, films . . . everywhere, everything a potential image, or the simulation of another image, everyone a producer and consumer of images.

She caught another glimpse of her rain-spotted reflection in the window as she lit a Marlboro Light. It wasn't the products made by westies she consumed as much as images, the images of products. She flipped through a fashion magazine in her mind, thinking how they made the body a billboard for designers' images. She inhaled deeply, painfully.

The smoke collided with the window, flattened out and dissipated in the open air of the apartment. No product epitomized the consumption of images more than film. Albert may have meant well when he sent her to the agent, but was he so naive to think that the agent wouldn't try to consume me? Adina asked herself, watching a car moving down the street, recalling the agent's words: "Do you think I'll get you a contract without seeing your legs? That's it, lift your skirt a little higher. Lovely. Now, come over here to the couch."

Where did I end up with my pride still intact? Applying ampules of chemicals to the skin of rich old women, like the mayor's wife who thinks I'm Polish, at the beauty salon in Schmargendorf. The rain was letting up, sprinkling in a fine mist. I have to get out, go to a museum and see people, or, she thought, go back to the east—back to gemeinschaft[23] relations. Adina dropped the half-smoked cigarette in her barely touched tea.

---

[23]  Community and the sociology category reflecting personal interactions and related values.

Adorned in silk threads and the fur-trimmed black leather coat given to her by Albert, she pushed through the building door into the street. A shop window reflected her half-shave Berlin bob glistening with gel. She exuded the cool, introverted indifference of westies, but she felt, in doing so, as though she were inside the skin of her nonexistent twin. She was, nonetheless, eager to make a good impression and couldn't suppress a smile to the downstairs neighbor as she passed him.

"Hello."

"Hello."

She recognized his scent, even in the open air. He had given her refuge one night when she and Albert were fighting. She recalled that night—how misled and abused she felt, despite the fact that she was the masochist's torturer. Somehow she couldn't help think that the neighbor's smile had more to do with Albert's screams than any act of friendship—she hadn't failed to see the traces of condescension on his lips, whatever the cause. The drama of that night wasn't a drama; it was, she had decided, reality. And it was Albert's fault.

Her boots marched down the street. If he had gone with me to see the casting agent, I would've achieved the status I deserve, Adina reassured herself. I can act and don't need classes—the erotic videos show that.

The wet wind seemed to pass through her. She wanted the warm comfort of old friends, the women from her former job near Tierpark and even some of the customers. The training at the fancy salon where she now worked actually interested her—aromatherapy, foot reflexology, lymph massage. But she was seen as just a sales clerk, a poor little creature from the east. No one even asked her to model anymore, although plenty of rich guys wanted to fuck—that much she knew. If she stayed in the west she would have to have a craft, something creative that was hers. Maybe fashion design, she thought, as we did in school, only now with fabric made with little holes like a woman's skirt she once saw in the train—a yellow skirt with holes that offered a glimpse at her semi-transparent panties: a glimpse of a glimpse.

Neither of the women she'd worked with had a phone, so all she could do was hope they were home. She put her head down and marched the short distance to the subway. The near empty station provided shelter from the rain, but it was still cold on the platform. Waiting for the train, she turned up her fur collar, which was brushing against her chin—it reminded her how Albert gave her nearly every luxury.

"When my girlfriends from the old salon see me, they'll think I've got the world at my feet," she whispered to herself. She tapped her toes. "Albert gives me all I want . . . except power—the power I felt when I was with Richard."

The heads of passersby turned but quickly turned back toward the tunnel where a train headlight approached. The sound of braking on metal tracks. The English name 'Dick' was now how she sometimes thought of Richard. The train stopped; the doors opened. Listening to Wagner at Albert's place, the name had dawned on her. She took a seat, and as the train began to move, Adina's eyes were drawn to a woman in green, cork-lined sandals and purple socks. There were little triangular hole patterns in her tight pants—Adina admired her shapely ass, searching for tell-tale panty lines, she found them only deep in the crack. The woman was standing in front of Adina reading a wobbly copy of *Zitty* magazine. For the salon woman who had applied so many cellulite treatments, the sight of this juicy young butt was mesmerizing. It even smells nice, she thought, as the train eased to a stop and it waved before her nose.

Another thing disturbed Adina about Albert—how little she knew about Berlin and its decadent ways, the image of women wearing only pearls and high heels dancing with other women came to her mind. Albert had failed to show her enough of the Berlin underworld, which she longed for, even if it no longer existed as it did in postcards from the interwar years when people went to private nightclubs, snorted cocaine and danced tango all night long.

The one thing Albert did show her—how to tell the types of prostitutes—indicated more than passive knowledge. The boot women reflected their specialty by the color of their footwear; the grasshoppers who didn't have room money and did it in parks; the gravestones with missing limbs and other deformities; the five o'clock ladies who did it after their day job. On their way around Berlin he would point out teams of mothers and of-age daughters and the Polish Jews with pageboy hair he said advertised as masseuses or worked as table-ladies in nightclubs.

At least Richard took the time to teach her about communal life, she thought, with his water polo teammates. It was an experience she could never forget. Richard and his friends seemed so vital, if not at times grisly. Compared to being with those colossal killers, she felt terribly old when she sat with Albert at the cashew counter of Harry's New York Bar on a Friday night, talking about how a streetwalker in green and gold shoelaces meant shit-smeared enslavement was being offered. There was so much else happening, that much she knew. He was a masochistic square who would have to get someone else, she thought, some other little eastern whore to supply his flagellation and discipline. The train surfaced, momentarily, giving her a glimpse of riveted iron pylons and graffiti remains on a concrete wall: FLIPPER, METACRATS, GOODBYE LA.

# CHAPTER 10

To a donkey, straw is more valuable than gold, the hotel clerk reminded himself, silently repeating this Heraclitean quip, as he did every morning, when he woke in his bed of straw. Typically also thinking of himself as an ass. Thanks to the American women, he'd moved into the squat basement so he could save money for his trip to Paris or Saint Petersburg.

Jan pulled at the straw on his belly and clawed his navel with a dirty fingernail. The light of dawn from the narrow window, intermittently interrupted by the legs of passersby on the sidewalk. He sat up and fumbled on the concrete floor for his glasses. Two fat crabs were buried in his skin: red, blood-swollen, like cancerous moles that frayed at the edges. They traveled from his pubes during the night by pulling themselves along the line of hair on his stomach.

You might as well start drinking, he thought, maybe sell blood and get drunk more easily. An empty liter of Zubrówka was perched on the wooden table next to a teacup and a stack of manuscript pages. Dried strands of bison grass coiled in the bottom of the bottle as metaphors for his twisted narrative. His prized Waterman ballpoint, made in France, was as close as he could get to writing in Paris.

Your eyes worsen with every letter, he thought. Like parasites, these letters suck your blood. All for what? So a cynical book pusher can make a killing on you once you're dead. He lifted his body off the floor, slipping into his soiled uniform as he hunched over, rising with his head amid the pipes hanging from the low ceiling. He moved to his desk and looked out the door across the hall.

Elsewhere in the squats, lovely Anne closed her eyes and simultaneously pulled a pen across paper as if submerged in a pool of ink. The jet-black lines were extensions of her head, like strands of her voluptuous hair. Impulses surged from her inner eye, through her ganglia, to her hand. The crude rays were an entry in her dream journal made while daybreak danced across her closed lids and animated her sketches with the phantasms of her senses—sinuous streams of ink reflecting lines projected on her backlit lids . . . black illuminations of memories of her sister walking the street, her senile father who pushed her mother to drugs.

Unlike her oblique approach to art, her blind lines, Anne met life head-on, shaping it to her will when she could. She dropped a broken strand of hair through the lusterless light shining in the round window set in her egg-shaped lattice of bent wood and wire painted with plaster. She had replaced the room's angles with curves to draw deeper from her well of feminine sensuality. Eyes again closed, the path of the pen took her back to school at the Berlin Institute of Architecture where an orderly amphitheater fluxed into tangled bacchanal.

She thought of Henrick, a passionate student who lived what he studied but rarely studied what he was told. A circular image of light formed behind her lids recalling the energy

Henrick had for whatever it was that impassioned him: the plan Bohigas drew up and realized to open up the medieval core of Barcelona or the delirious deconstructivist architecture of Koolhaas.

Her memory pool rippled into the image of her fellow students on the floor of Zoo Station . . . an obscure corner at the confluence of a cargo warehouse manned by indolent workers and several rows of lockers. A pallet jack rolled across the concrete floor, pushed by a swarthy man in overalls, toward piles of boxes under the signs WIEN, ROTTERDAM, HAMBURG. The smell of burnt butane gas from the forklift.

At that time, Henrick lived around town—home, hotels, dorm rooms, squats in the east and west—so he kept clothes in a locker at the station. None of the artists spotted him. As he changed clothes by the locker, he changed his mind and stepped on the baggage scale, nude in a pose reminiscent of a Greek sculpture.

The titillated laughter, the flurry of pencils, the howls of station workers, the interest of passersby, then of the police. Anne played out the scene several ways, feeling at home in Hell because it was the perfect place to create her wild architecture. She thrived on the loose consensual morality that was tolerant of anomie—a situation of intimacy and trust, particularly in what she called her Circle of Confusion.

Anne pushed aside her drawing board and put the paper under her legs. The concave mirror of a broken automobile headlight was on her nightstand. She brought it next to her labia—the distorted lips and tender opening reflected in the jagged glass perilously close to her slender thighs . . . the last image before she again closed her eyes. She dropped the mirror and probed herself.

Finger painting with menstrual fluid: the doors to long, dark, serpentine labyrinths—like tubes or intestines in the core of her body. And when she opened her eyes, Henrick was at the round door. Curly blond hair, a face that looked chiseled out of marble, brawny shoulders—he was at that age when confidence and ability coincide, seemingly giving him the power to consummate anything he initiated.

Anne sensed his presence and opened her eyes. Was that memory of him . . . my drawing . . . a premonition he would come? She asked herself this and other questions in disbelief as she beckoned him to come with an outstretched arm and open legs. Henrick eyed the broken headlight.

"Did you cut yourself?"

"No, it was a full moon last night," she said as the glass fell off the mattress with a clink.

Henrick thought of himself as the man with the finest taste, which was reflected in his choice of mate—lovely Anne—and in what he wanted to taste. He naturally wanted her honey as he thought of her secretions, but this time of month he also wanted what was most worth tasting on his tongue: her wine-red blood tinged with the taste of her piss coursing with vitality that moistened his soul with her soul as their spirits came together as blood brother and sister.

Jan turned back to his writing desk, picked up his pen: Piss is the blood of life that she lets every place, every day, he wrote, and blood was the water of her soul that she lets just once a month. He glanced at his watch and recalled the hotel clerk job, suddenly going into action by stuffing his shaving kit, clean shirt and underwear in a battered Naugahyde attaché case. These parasites are a nuisance, but more than that, an expense. Not only do I support the razor industry, but now the pharmaceutical companies. That's what you get for your risky behavior—you'll wind up with hepatitis or tuberculosis with the drug addicts in this joint .

Banging sounds on the pipes, but there was still no water in the walls. He stood up, ready for a rubber room; anything other than this hellhole. Only the beauty of his text and daydreams of Paris consoled him. Drifting from Saint Denis to Clichy like Brando in *Last Tango*. Nights of agitation—no power to sleep—with mental messages from my dead wife. The hazards of bachelor life: fallen women, strippers, whores . . . passionless encounters with pebble hearts, so small and hard.

Jan closed the door to Hell and stepped into Berlin's blue haze. He shot a glance at a striking woman across the street on the steps of the Alter Native squat. She was speaking with a Turk, a well-known guy in the neighborhood. But she looked vaguely familiar, as if he knew her from somewhere else, like a word on the tip of his tongue—a total impression of an expression with the inability to fully differentiate and articulate it. She didn't notice him.

On his way to the subway, Jan reminded himself to stop for medicine at the pharmacy. He walked with his head down, watching his feet plod along the concrete, thinking how he disliked his job. And even though he was an atheist, he hated working Sundays more than other days. As he pushed through the pharmacy door, he noticed how some of the products from the west were already lining the shelves in their brightly colored packaging. The section specializing in sexual commodities— condoms, pregnancy tests, lubricating gels—was well known to him. He found a bottle of lice shampoo and headed over to the cashier, with whom he empathized for having to work on the weekend. She has the look of a fellow Pole in her green eyes, he thought, and that straight nose and those soft lips.

"I like your scarf," he said.

She glanced up from the specialized shampoo. "Thank you. I use it to strangle lousy guys like you."

"You're a sassy one, aren't you?"

"Just be careful when you use this product—it contains lindane, which goes through your skin and can damage your brain and nerves. No more than four minutes contact."

Jan looked at the box, not sure if she was kidding.

"Next," she said.

He turned away with a smile, thinking she was local, which was fine as he loved how German women expressed their passion, their burning and reflexive sense of it. If he had wanted to see a Polish woman in her, it was because he missed his mother and sisters. And in Poland, he had at least been able defend his writing time on the so-called Lord's Day, whereas in Germany he had to work. He passed umbrella-covered tables along the tree-lined sidewalk, then crossed a brick plaza and followed a curved railing into the subway.

While reading the latest *A-Infos* on the platform, he also read the minds of those around him . . . people working hard at enjoying their leisure. Luckily, there were no faschos[24] around. In the near empty train, Jan took a pull on the vodka bottle. Every piece he read about the strikes and protests was accompanied by his imagined voice-over from fellow passengers, as if their sounds hovered between the text and his eyes: "You wouldn't last a minute without a government. Who would protect you?" It's the same with women, he thought, if I renounce them, it only makes me vulnerable to episodes like the one with those lousy Americans. What did I drink last night? A few mugs at the hotel, a few shots in Hell.

---

[24]  Fascists.

Reading was hopeless, a reminder that he too was a victim of domination, being dominated by his additions and other writers' thoughts. No thought of resistance other than slipping off the margins of society into the squat. The train surfaced in the rain, projecting shadows of water-beads on the face of a lady wearing cat's eye glasses that accentuated her feline features. The copy of Walter Serner's story collection *At the Blue Monkey* in her lap, along with her stirrup pants, pointed ankle boots and a blue silk blouse that hinted at a luxurious sense of aesthetics.

If you didn't reek of booze, you could go over to her, Jan told himself. Or I could tell her I drink for the state of euphoria that is otherwise unattainable given the absence of the anarchist nonstate. Jan moved to the forward door, glancing back at her in the window as the train pulled to a stop. The reflections of their eyes met in the rain-spotted glass. He doubled back, sidestepped a brawny worker headed the other way, and stumbled into the empty seat behind her. The train lurched forward.

"I'm sorry," Jan began, leaning over the back of her seat, "but it's hard for me to find people who share my taste in literature—I just finished rereading that book."

She smiled to conceal her shock. The alcohol made his accent less than perfect and, at that hour, no Berliner would speak to her that gently.

"For me," he went on, "our meeting could be a scene from that book: the public space—a subway car, for example— recalls private memories. You know, was once reading the same Böll as the woman next to me in the train."

"Don't expect me to take her place," the woman advised.

"I'm terribly sorry." Jan shook his head. "I simply wanted to say that I can identify with narratives that put personal experiences in the physical reality of public places like Serner's café-bars or this subway car."

"From the looks of you, well, you might have some of the same existential dilemmas as Serner's characters," she said.

A nearby passenger put on his headphones to tune out the conversation.

"I was in fact thinking of the freedom that can be found in a situation," Jan said, "after Satre. Are you a philosopher?"

She raised her book. "I'm into literature."

"At a high level."

She opened the book and began to read.

"You probably wouldn't believe that I had a bar in London named after that book."

She glanced up. "You owned a bar in London?"

"No, it was named at my suggestion."

"You're right," she said, "I probably wouldn't believe it."

Jan smiled. "I admire your skepticism."

"I'm not a philosopher." She got up to go.

"That's what all the real philosophers say," he said as she walked away.

They exchanged glances in the glass for an instant as the train pulled into Wagner Platz. The door opened and she was gone. If she had liked you, he thought, if you'd been sober, you'd be on your way to a café with her and a true sense of emancipatory consciousness in your head instead of heading to work. As the train rumbled through the rain, Jan saw the light in a room near the tracks and his face in the train window . . . bent over an Olympia typewriter in an otherwise empty room. The cold realization that life was passing him by. A catwoman, perhaps an *ultraphilosophe*, had come into his life and left in the blink of an eye.

*

At the Alex, in the basement of the State Hotel, a maid with classic features—her blond hair in a tight, thick braid—lifted the clerk's lice-infested clothing by a mop handle into the washer. Piece by piece: shreds of socks, lousy briefs, wilted gray trousers and a matching jacket—one of his two white shirts.

The dirty ring around his collar, like the quicksilver rings in the maid's ears, belied the incompatibility of their counterfeit signs with the reality of their existence. This unnatural dissociation of workers and their class was mirrored in the spiritless transformation to the new system underway at the State Hotel where the view of the future bordered on indifference, as if it would certainly be dull. Perhaps this was understandable on the part of the maid. As for the clerk, the partisan of becoming, he longed to transcend his class and for the passions he imagined in faraway places—he was just a bit jaded from having been there too long.

He was also infested, and not simply with crabs. Early in his stay in Berlin, he read a subversive little book that had been written over a century ago by one of the city's less illustrious inhabitants: Max Stirner, who spent more than his fair share of time in debtors' prisons. Initially, Jan, the student of languages, was struck by the author's German etymology in *The Ego and His Own*, which showed how pre-Christian meanings opposed the present denotations of words—an insult was merely a jest; impudence was bravery, and so on.

As he probed deeper, imagining this Young Hegelian in the company of Bakunin and Marx, he was moved by the undulating intensity of Stirner's anarchistic style: "Am I my own when I give myself up to sensuality? No, I must master sensuality." Jan asked himself that question as he washed himself with acrid lice shampoo in the mop sink.

Despite Jan's elastic ego that was subject to contractions during more introspective moments, the little book exalting the expansive ego left a trace. If I were a true Stirnerian, he silently said to himself, I wouldn't let my enjoyment of life be stolen through labor, least of all by the State Hotel. I would tell the state to get out of his sunshine.

Yet in consuming himself creatively, he was true to the credo of the book—the egoistic purpose of writing raised him above society while allowing him to have intercourse with it; this creativity was the signpost of salvation in a meaningless world—the way to obtain value from himself—even if it only led to the dirty back alleys of culture.

In fairness to the clerk, he realized his pauperism was due to his lack of value, that he and his type were as much to blame for the rich as the rich were for the poor. It was within his competence to take a room in Hell, but it was beyond him to stop drinking.

He stripped off the last of his clothes and turned back to the mop sink. His head throbbed. The cold water will do me good. He bent at the waist. There's nothing to be learned from drinking, he said to himself in a whisper that was drowned in the cold water, which felt like an ice pick in the front of his skull.

"Here, take this," the maid said listlessly.

She handed him a towel from the linen shelves lining the wall, indifferent to his naked body, as if it were another mop in the sink.

"I really appreciate your help," he said.

Seeing the maid this way, Jan realized that he slept with most women he met. Not that he tried, it just happened. How many times had he looked around a room—say, at a party—and shocked himself with the fact that several of the women in attendance had been his lovers? Too many. He always held to the illusion that one would lead to romantic love, whereas, in reality, he knew he was a slave to sensuality because it made him happy and he owned up to this knowledge.

"Wash again tonight to make sure you kill them," the maid ordered. After a pause, she added, "They carry diseases with them, you know?"

"I know," Jan said despondently as he wrapped a towel around his waist.

"Don't get mad at me."

"I'm not. It's just . . ." He looked for the words to defend his actions while putting his glasses on his nose. "It's just that I'm upset that this happened."

"Here, sit down and have a cup of coffee while your uniform is in the wash."

Jan followed her to the credenza where the maids brewed coffee, and when she turned to hand him a cup, he kissed her forehead.

"None of that here," another maid laughed as she entered the room. "You're still looking good, Jan."

A shiver ran down his spine. Not another lover, he thought, turning to put a face on the voice.

"Good morning to you," he said.

They moved to the table and took first sips when a bellboy stepped into the room.

"Jan, I've been looking for you. Some westie producer is filming in the rooms—a documentary on prostitutes. He just asked if we had a stud for his film. We thought of you. What do you think? It'd be the first time you got paid to fuck a whore."

"Don't be so sure," the second maid—a buxom, middle-aged brunette to whom Jan had given passion out of generosity—replied for Jan. "For all you know, pimps send him their prospects to make sure their muffs are up to snuff."

"How much?" Jan asked, cutting to the quick.

"He mentioned something about it," the bellboy said, "but you'd better talk to him."

Jan tried to ignore the first maid's scowl and the second maid's unwelcome compliment.

"I asked how much," Jan said, noticing the bellboy's disconcerting nervousness

"He said he'd pay the right guy five hundred marks."

Jan ran his fingers through his hair to make it stick out. "Tell him I'll be right up and tell whoever's on duty that I'll cut him in if he covers for me."

"Room 1699," the bellboy said as backed out the door.

"How can you?" the young maid asked, more as a friend than a lover.

"How else will I get to Paris?" He spoke over the brim of his cup. "From now on, if anyone wants my respect, he or she will have to pay for it."

*

Scrubbed, disinfested, dressed in his freshly washed uniform, Jan felt like a new man, only with the same old bad conscience. The journey to a guest room reminded him of the pretty young woman and the disgusting Stasi agents. Jan knocked and the door opened on a man whose consciousness was on the lookout for the next image. His sex worker turned actress was standing behind him, smoking.

Through the round lenses of his horn-rimmed glasses, Jan took her in from head to toe: she had big blond hair that swept to one side and fell down her back; tiny daggers dangling from her ears; a look of sexual confidence in her amber eyes; features that seemed carved out of wood; a gold-studded, leather collar and shoulderpad combo with chains that looped through eyelets along the edges—down her shoulder, across her chest; and matching panties—the gold chains forming concentric curves from her buns, around her hips, to her crotch. With her arms crossed under jutting breasts, breasts tipped with golden pasties, her wedding band was in plain view. And below, spiked rubber boots with laces up the front.

Charlotte touched her middle finger to her lips: "I guess he'll do."

"That's for me to decide," Albert said, raising his voice in a way that made him seem decisive. He shook Jan's hand and asked, "You've agreed to the fee?"

"Yes, provided I can wear a condom."

"No problem," Albert said with a wave of the hand. "I'd like you to have sex with her for the sake of realism, but don't worry, I won't be on my hands and knees zooming in on your genitals. No, no, I have something different in mind." He motioned toward the bed. "Have a seat. My name is Albert and this is Charlotte."

"Johann," Jan lied.

The clerk bowed at the waist toward her, shook Albert's hand again, took a seat.

"I'll be right back, I just have to use the toilet," Albert excused himself, then turned back and added: "If you could get ready."

Jan pulled at the laces to his black leather shoes and kicked them off while looking around the room: a typical suite, with the exception of the video camera on a tripod and the presence of this lioness.

"You must be good at what you do," Jan ventured.

"I'm a pro. Some of my clients say I'm the best. You'll find out soon enough."

She squinted at Jan through the smoke of the cigarette clenched between her teeth. Jan stood up and stripped to the waist under Charlotte's gaze. By her attire, he guessed that this meant a great deal to her. Free advertising or her big break in show business. Why else would she be so interested in the way I look? Jan dropped his trousers, revealing his sausage.

"Hmm, you surprise me," Charlotte said as he walked to the window.

He knew that he still had his form, which he'd developed as a teen when bullies and jocks picked on him, not so much for his size as his eyes. They stole his glasses and turned him into an easy target. Otherwise he wouldn't have bothered to lift weights, he was too studious. He practiced these power moves through his early twenties, calling them his "fucking exercises." Unlike those who were swept up by the bodybuilding craze, Jan's power moves put his entire body behind the weight, his lower back, his hips and particularly his largest muscle, his ass.

Charlotte and Jan stared at one another across the room as he leaned against the wall with his shoulder; she smoked, looking out the window at the rain-swept city from skyscraper height. From her profile, Jan knew he had met his match—she had beautiful breasts, such touchable flesh, but her ass was truly something to reckon with.

Albert, meanwhile, was in the rest room washing his hands. When it came down to it, the director felt queasy being in a shoddy hotel room with naked strangers. He felt dirty, although he shouldn't have given his experience with erotic video clubs—experience that he intended to capitalize on here. He dried his hands and emerged with a firm plan in mind.

"I want you two to face the TV." Albert glanced at the screen flickering with news and felt reassured—the whole world was dirty. "I'll play the interviews on the VCR and film them over your bodies. Everything will be in frame and you'll have plenty of room to maneuver." He pressed play by remote and turned up the volume so that they could barely hear him over the static hiss of the leader. "Just do whatever comes naturally, but try not to make much noise because I want to get the interviews on the sound track with one shot—a few groans would be nice, but no talking. Okay?"

"Yes," Jan said.

Charlotte stamped out her smoke and silently sprawled across the bed wearing a smile she'd worn so many times before. Albert checked the viewfinder and made a sign to them. A red light appeared on the camera as the angular face of a seemingly nude woman filled the television screen.

"My name is Susanna. I became a prostitute when my husband left me. What else could I do? I have a daughter to feed."

Jan watched Susanna's lips move on the screen and tried to imagine the number of men who'd enjoyed them. She had a hard face, but soft eyes. Albert waved for Jan to go to work. Charlotte's meaty flank swathed in chains caught the eye of the camera, her coifed and combed pussy fur, her breasts that stuck up as she lay back, her fluffy blond locks spread over the bed.

Jan began slowly untying her rubber boots. Comical tugs exaggerated for the camera. The boots fell to the floor. She purred as he licked her feet, not expecting such treatment. What a lovely surprise, she thought as she involuntarily locked her hands behind her head, let out a sigh and looked past her armpit at the four-eyed man who paid so much attention to her. She giggled at the tickling sensation on her toes and her hips rocked slightly from one bun to the other.

Susanna's voice filled the room: "I have to work every day just to live. There's more money at the massage parlors that have opened up since the wall came down, but I haven't been able to find a job in one. As it is, I walk the streets and take my dates to a hotel that caters to our trade. The clients? They're all the same. So long as they pay."

Jan ran his tongue up Charlotte's calf. It seemed she'd never shaved, yet there was only the lightest fuzz growing on her sumptuous skin. He was reassured by her laughter as his spiky hair tickled her, and by the melting tension in her legs. It was as if she were actually vulnerable to enjoying herself.

"I don't like to fuck in cars because I can't wash myself and it's really bad if semen gets on the seat," Susanna continued. "If a john really wants to fuck in his car, he has to wear a rubber. If not, nothing. Most guys want blowjobs in their cars anyway. I always bring a bottle of mouthwash with me to clean my mouth . . ."

Jan nibbled and kissed the length of Charlotte's thighs, blowing light puffs of hot air through the chains, under the edge of her leather thong. Higher, in the middle of her smooth stomach, he stuck his tongue in her navel, tickling her even more than before, showing her what he would do to her clitoris if she weren't a sex worker. She raked her nails across his back.

Another voice, high and fast, came from the television: "Hi, I'm Inseln. All I can tell you is that you can't make anything here. Those foreigners get all the clients. Life's shitty. Before the fall of the wall, things were better. Competition? Give people a little freedom and everyone wants to be a whore. But what really gets me are those daughters of foreign bitches who only have shit and syphilis."

# CHAPTER 11

Jackboots on cobblestones in the afternoon. Harsh marching sounds reminiscent of brownshirts wearing red, white and black armbands emblazoned with the notorious Hindu symbol used by the National Socialist German Workers Party. They came from the nearby bar, the Happen, and other points in East Berlin: skinheads armed with firebombs, guns, knives and telephone cable.

Hypnotized by violence and their cultist awe for their führer, they moved down streets scarred from previous battles with the autonomes and police: dislodged stones, trenches, remains of barricades, a charred car. The skins were reassured by the brute presence of four former Stasi.

"They better follow their own advice." The neonazi leader pointed to the graffiti on the squat: LEARN TO BURN, ARM YOURSELF, LIFE BEGINS WHERE THE STATE ENDS.

Richard's massive body flinched. "The state ends . . . the state ends . . ." echoed in his mind. "Life begins . . . life begins . . ." Saltwater welled up in his eyes; a radio in his pocket crackled.

"Richard, come in Richard."

He brought the microphone to his whiskers. "Richard here. Go ahead, Gerrit."

"Ready when you are."

"Hans, how about you? In position?"

"Yeah. We'll be back in the Aquadrome in no time."

"We have to catch them by surprise," Richard said.

"You can't be serious," the Nazi protested. "We've got more firepower."

"Remember, that's my flat up there. Don't torch it."

"No worries, this will just be a little storm trooper sports festival. Happy to have you on my team."

The Nazi extended his hand; Richard acted as if he didn't see it.

"Let's do it," Richard said into the radio.

"Yeah." The leader took a swig of colorless korn. "Let's displace these 'displaced' people."

They charged ahead, firing the first shot by smashing a parked car window with a piece of telephone cable. Breakaway glass broke away. The leader felt crushed bits under his boot and smiled.

In the occupied building, two autonome women knocked at the door of the old woman who had lived there for years. She was glad the kids had come because she felt threatened being there alone; she gave the young women cigarettes. Hadid and Mohawk fetched coal from the basement. A big, round guy made kindling by placing sticks in an iron chair where a seat once was and by stomping on them. On an upper floors, an anarchist dandy and two runaways, one with a tubercular cough, watched a television with a bricolage antenna tuned to an absurd game show. In the next room, adorned with pictures women love to hate, a man slept away a difficult day after a long night of hard drinking.

Two skins scaled the backyard fence and hustled across the courtyard. One lit the Molotov and the other threw it at a third story window. It bounced off a makeshift grate made from a grocery cart and fell to the ground. Fire splashed in the courtyard.

Speed metal music ground to a halt as a peroxide-blond punk swept the courtyard with a spotlight and strands of light brushed the skins back over the fence. The fascho alarm sounded, along with screams from a choir of women who at one time or another had been crushed by fascist boots.

Hadid dropped the buckets of coal and rushed up the steps from the cellar—slipped on dogshit in the entrance, regained his balance. He threw himself on the main door, twisted the deadbolts shut. With Mohawk's help, they inserted a beam of wood in the brackets on the door.

"The Nazis were run out," Hadid yelled. "But their grandchildren are back."

The kids who tried to live in harmony with self-law took their security posts. A big guy with orange hair and a cutting hangover rushed past the anarchist orgy. He looked down on the street through a grocery cart grate in the window as something sizzled past his ear—a blast of gunfire from the skins trying to bust in the door, drilling a hole in the bottom part of the door with bullets as the young autonome women peeled slates off the roof with their blue nails and pitched them from the roof as if playing a cruel adolescent game.

"Not like that," one of the women said. "Watch me."

"Oh, you hit one."

From the kitchen door, the Rap Assassin, as he called himself, had been half-listening to Jutte discuss their nonhierarchical relationship with reality and other recondite subjects with other autonome women: "Why can't we make art, or at least tee shirts?" "No, we're trying to negate commodities and spectacles." "Who are you to say what we can or can't do?" "Nobody. As I said before: power to workers' councils." "Yeah, but there's not an honest prole among us—least of all you." "I don't want power . . . how could I since I don't want to work." "Shots!" The women made for boxes of bottles. The Rap Assassin pulled out a revolver.

"Stay back." Hadid pressed against the wall next to the door—he was yelling to the red-haired punk with two dogs on chains in one hand and a club in the other.

The punk chained his dogs to the stairwell at the landing. "We can't let them past the first floor. Hadid, get up here, the door's about to go."

The door was riddled with bullet holes and shot-off locks. The only thing holding them together was the raw timber beam that spanned the door and its frame. It bulged with every lunge by the skins and Stasi athletes. A firebomb slipped through a hole in the door, broke on the marble floor; it erupted in a wall of flames that blocked the stairs from Hadid.

He climbed atop the wrought-iron elevator cage and shimmied up the cables as dogs howled at the fire and smoke, choking themselves on their chains. Straddling the stairway banister with the help of the red-haired punk, Hadid lifted himself over the rail and turned to the source of a cracking sound just as a little car plowed through the doorway, stopping short of the fire in the entrance.

The rapper nodded to Hadid. With one hand gripping the elevator cable, the musician leapt over the first floor banister and slid down, firing at the shattered windshield. He nailed the driver. The passenger crawled out of the car under cover of smoke and fire: he was a burly skin covered with tattoos and armed with a bayonet on the end of the stolen AK-47. The rapper fired his last shot as the skin came after him. It missed. The burly skin clawed his way up the elevator cage with one hand, and with a great last heave, stabbed the rapper in the gut with his gun and pulled the trigger.

In a rage, Mohawk pulled out his good knife, a Big Swede, but wavered when he saw the reinforcements squeeze through the hole created by the car: the lanky skin and his pals, two ex-Stasis from the water polo team. Luckily for Mohawk, he was held back by Hadid.

"The dogs will slow them down on the stairs, and they're covering the cables." Hadid pointed to the autonome women pelting the burly skin with bottles. "Let's make a barricade with everything we've got."

# CHAPTER 12

❀

Jan glanced at the face of the next sex worker as she appeared on the television—hard, angular, framed by blond hair that darkened at the roots. He didn't catch her name. His gaze moved to the purple spandex top crisscrossing her tits and wrapping around her shoulders . . . mother-of-pearl stones on a silver bead necklace nestled in the groove between jutting globes. Her glossy lips issued a weak laugh at something off camera.

"You'd never believe what some of those industrialists want," she said. "If only their employees could see the bigwig's bald head between my thighs. Rare requests? What you call rare isn't so rare. I don't like working with a transvestite, but it pays well. After playing around in bed a little we make a sandwich: me on the bottom, the client in the middle and the transvestite on him—you can imagine."

Jan checked with his tongue for implant scars along the underside of Charlotte's impressive breasts, breasts that stood up even as she lay back. His tonguetip dabbed her luscious flesh, moving higher on the curved, filmy surface. He circled both areolas in a figure eight, then gripped a golden pastie with his teeth and pulled it off: the faint taste of dried glue for him; a feminine ouch from her. His tongue slid over her half-hard papilla that grew to full length between his nursing lips. Charlotte shifted her back on the bed and ran her hands through Jan's spiky hair; she gasped despite herself as electric current streamed through her body.

"Hello, my name is Lisa."

Jan watched out of the corner of his eye as a stunning brunette filled the screen; she swayed out of view and back as she settled in her seat. Meanwhile he fingered Charlotte's bulbous breasts mounds of flesh that felt on the verge of bursting against his greedy palms. The television screen suffused them in a soft glow.

"I've been doing this for about six months," Lisa began. "The first time was really difficult, but I needed the money for an abortion. There are worse things in life, and in this line of work, there are worse ways to go about it. I only work with referrals. After my abortion, I didn't think I'd do it again, but then I couldn't find a job. Drugs? I've tried them all but don't sell them. All I can tell you is that it's better to be a whore than to be broke."

A glazed, distant look—as if she were on drugs—came over Charlotte's eyes as Jan straightened his glasses. He admired the lilt of her breast for a hands-free instant; she arched an eyebrow, then closed her eyes as she felt his passionate hands again encircle her tits, then roam over her ribs, down her curved waist and hips. She turned on her side and offered him her rump. His sensuous fingers raked a fleshy white sphere and gripped it, reaching for the depths of her body while reddening the luxuriously smooth surface. Her ass reared up in his hand and pressed between his claws.

Here it is, baby—he moved his hips to her face and wedged his pole between her lips; they slowly parted for the camera as the swelling glans stretched back and each vein-bulging segment invaded her mouth. Her nostrils flared, her eyes closed. And looking down on her now, Jan combed her fluffy hair first back on the side and then under the back of her head. She felt tingling sensations from nails grazing her scalp—they traveled up her head and raced down her spine.

She shivered. That's good, he thought. You must know that I want you to like it. With his free hand, he pulled her leather collar so her face pressed into his balls. She kissed and gently sucked one and then the other. Jan raised his sac and then pressed his penile artery against her nose, she inhaled deeply. Jan hooked Charlotte's lips and undulated on her tongue. Savoring the sensation, he gritted "yes" through clenched teeth—Albert raised his finger to his lips for Jan to be quiet while the next sex worker appeared on the screen.

"It started when I worked as a waitress. I was friends with one of the customers . . . he wanted to become better friends. Like a fool, I went to his flat. I was only nineteen and he was very smooth. Silly me. There wasn't much light and before I knew it, he put my hand on his penis. It was soft and hard at the same time. He told me to move my hand up and down, and I did it. Then he kissed me everywhere and undressed me at the same time. We did everything a man and woman can do together. It was my first time. When I left with a fortune in my pocket, I felt some shame, but looking back on it, there was nothing bad about the man. He was a classic man of money. When he meets an inexperienced young woman, he initiates her in all the things he likes. That man led to another and another. Where will it end? I'd go to an asylum if they'd have me. Otherwise, I'll end up in the morgue. Now I don't care what a man does to me—anything he likes—so long as he pays."

Albert tore open a condom and threw it on the bed for Jan. "So long as he pays . . . so long as he pays," echoed in Jan's ears along with Charlotte's muffled groans.

# CHAPTER 13

Above ground in the black east, Adina walked away from the subway and noticed most of the factories were still closed on Sundays. She inhaled deeply, thinking the air in the west lacked the same alkalinity. Car tires rippled over cobblestones. She passed a man who smelled of tobacco, and then some kittenish young women speaking about fashion. Many factories, she knew, were now closed every day as the unemployed masses numbly resigned themselves to being second-class Germans. At least they have the Berliner Luft[25] to breathe, she thought, but who knows how long that will last. We survived socialism and the Stasi—Adina had a mix of pride and disgust as she eyed rows of western billboards—but will we be able to survive capitalism?

She took long strides on the empty sidewalk, walking in afternoon darkness between streetlights. Some things had changed, but she felt as though she had changed more: the east in her had, in part, been negated by the west, but as she came

---

[25]  Berlin Air; the phrase was a song title.

back east via subway to familiar streets, the west was in turn partially negated as well. In this tamping down and welling up of feeling about her hometown, the changeable changed and the rest of her personality advanced through changing contexts. A streetlight cast shadows of Adina on the concrete before her. She turned a corner and walked up the car-lined walk into a semidemolished, deserted atmosphere, each step forward taking her back. She turned again onto a once familiar street. Richard was dodging slates in front of the communal flat and a car wedged in the doorway.

"Richard," she yelled. "What's going on?" Richard saw her. "Adina, be careful. Stay back."

She was driven to him—her body tingled with excitement, instantly awakened by Richard's size and power.

"Watch out!" she shrieked.

A slate chip nicked Richard's bald spot and blood ran through the closely cropped hair, down his neck.

"Fucking anarchists," Richard began. "The most dangerous hellcats in Berlin. They think they have a utopia here in our apartment building."

Adina dabbed the cut with tissue.

Richard clenched his teeth for an instant then went on: "You've probably seen their empty graffiti against exploitation. They don't understand the causes of exploitation—"

More slates fell, near misses that shattered on the concrete sidewalk.

"Easy," she said. "We better get out of here."

"And if they don't want power as they say," Richard continued, oblivious to Adina's advice, "then they are simply submitting to the will of bourgeois politicians like your mother."

Why did he bring up my mother? Adina wondered.

"Individualists!" Richard shouted with disgust to his assailants on the roof. "Subjectivists!"

He couldn't imagine that the runaways might be flattered by his insults.

"What do you have against my mother?" Adina asked.

"Nothing." Richard grabbed her arm, pulled her away from a falling slate. "Come on."

They went in, picking their way through the rubble created by the car. Adina glanced at the dead skin, his bloody head resting on the steering wheel. Her nipples stiffened. They carefully stepped into the smoky entrance where a grapple hook smashed through the stained glass window on the landing, sending the dogs into greater hysteria. Bottles broke against the walls—inaccurate shots by the bad women, aimed at the ex-Stasi who was climbing the elevator cable. The burly skin was pinned under a sofa and other furniture that formed a barricade on the stairs, his AK-47 now in the hands of Hadid. Hans lay in a heap of muscular flesh next to the rap assassin, on top of the wrought iron elevator.

Everything happened so quickly—almost simultaneously— that, to Adina, it was unreal, as if she had stepped into one of the underground comic strips anarchists pasted all over Berlin, like Nazi Raus[26]: "Bam, bof, biff, baf, pow, clack, aggg!" in speech bubbles over scenes of a dog swinging a fascist cat by its tail.

Jutte's bottle hit its target; Richard fell with a thud and the sound of his nylon jacket brushing the sooty floor. Hadid shot Gerrit in the neck; he lost his grip on the cable and started to fall. Coming from outside the squat, a skinhead suddenly pushed through the broken stained glass window. The dogs

---

[26] Get out.

bit into his legs and ripped his muscles with vicious jaws and teeth. He crumpled over and they tore into his gut and neck, snarling and twisting their powerful necks.

Everyone else retreated. Everyone except Adina who stood in shock, alone, at the mercy of these pitiless anarchists. Anarchists, she thought . . . the word made her shudder in revulsion as she ran her hands through Richard's bloodstained hair.

"Poor Richard," she murmured. "You just wanted your apartment."

She turned toward the movement of a handsome Turk with a Russian rifle in hand.

"Come with me," he said.

"No."

Hadid lowered the bayonet to her throat.

"I didn't have anything to do with this," Adina said.

"Then why are you here?"

"I was just passing . . ." she couldn't finish her phrase—the words about to issue from her lovely lips struck even her as unbelievable.

"I'll interrogate her in the coal room," Hadid said to Jutte and the others. "Let's see if we can mop this place up. Bury the dead."

Adina look up at Hadid. "What do you want from me?"

"All I want is the truth," Hadid said, as if reading her mind.

It was hard for Adina to believe, but then Hadid made her cease to believe herself. The truth was that the Turk seemed more domineering, more destructive, more deadly than Richard or any of his friends who had already raised the bar of masculinity on those counts to a high level. She had just witnessed the most direct and brutal violence of her young life, seen him kill with atrocious simplicity.

Hadid pulled her off the floor. "You have no reason to fear. Come."

Leading her by the hand, Hadid picked his way through the rubble and carnage, guided her down a narrow, steep stairwell. Adina hesitated. Hadid tugged at her hand. They stumbled over the half-empty buckets of coal Hadid had dropped during the assault and moved into the coal room. A diffused light cast on the dusty floor through a fairly large hole in the ceiling, a dim spotlight with irregular shadows from the broken rafters that made way for the rope lift and coal buckets.

"Sit down," Hadid ordered.

"But it's so dirty."

"Don't be prissy."

At that moment, Adina hated him more than anyone, anything, everything. Still, she felt a pleasant will to submit as she sat down on the floor and started to lean against the wall but remembered her hair, her new half-shave Berlin bob full of mousse. To hell with it, she thought and leaned back anyway.

"That's it," Hadid said, "make yourself comfortable. You seem a little shaken up. It's only natural. I don't feel very relaxed either. After all, we've both been through more or less the same thing. Nobody likes violence, except those fascist friends of yours. They live for it, don't they?" Without letting Adina agree, Hadid continued. "So you were just passing by? Likely story. You could make this easier on both of us if you simply . . ."

Adina was lost in the sound of Hadid's voice; it was as if a folkish umph pah played over tribal drums in a weird cacophony and she gave way to the overpowering dissonance. She looked up at his dark features that seemed darker in the shadows of the coal room. His face evoked for her the exoticism in art that had such erotic connotations.

"You shouldn't judge us harshly. Certainly we are entitled to the same leniency you grant yourself. We were only defending ourselves."

The seductive beat of his voice and the logic dictated that Adina mollify Hadid and gain release. She hadn't made a vow of silence with Richard and knew nothing about his current activities. They had been estranged for some time now. In a flash, she recalled the stabbing on the Linden, the dead Turk. He could be right. These anarchists were just defending themselves.

"I'll tell you anything you want to know. They killed a foreigner who tried to pick me up on the Linden. How's that for a confession? The ones I know were Stasi—about the others, I don't know."

"What are you to them—these Stasi?"

"I was, at one time, if you must know, their slut. I haven't seen them since the wall."

Hadid paced back and forth in front of the coal bins, his head flickering in and out of the light that encircled Adina.

"A Stasi slut, eh? Well, since there are no longer Stasis, that makes you an ex-Stasi slut. You'll have to become something else. Something better."

"I'm a Berliner, so I'm always ready for change," Adina said in a lilting voice.

"A Berliner? I'm a world citizen. Most everywhere else in Berlin, immigrants and natives live next to each other—here we live together. You're probably one of those people who think foreign culture ruins your Berlin." Hadid could see the deep impression he was making.

Adina thought for a moment. "I guess I . . ." She couldn't make this admission to the man she was falling for—it was as if she no longer thought that way. She didn't know anymore.

She didn't know herself. She had become foreign to herself and it had taken a foreigner to make her aware of it.

"Who are you?" Adina asked.

"Me? Hadid, commissar of enlightenment. Ah, you Germans . . . you can be so silly with your seriousness," Hadid said, affecting a high German accent. "You know, one thing that has always fascinated me about the German language is that the senses and sensuality, or, to be more precise, sense perception and sexual gratification, are both sinnlichkeit. You strike me as someone who has such powerful sinnlichkeit—smell, sight, touch, hearing—that you privilege intuition gained through the senses, what Kant called anschauung. I say this because the perfection of sensitive thought is beauty and you're beautiful."

Adina blushed at this blatant flattery.

"But what I'd like to know," Hadid said, "is if you're impulsive and playful enough to really get off sexually."

As an experiment, Hadid dropped his rifle. He neared her with a soft smile and placed a deep kiss on Adina's receptive lips. In the weak light, saliva glistened on her chin. She liked his smell: spicy, natural—not like Albert with his French toilette water or Richard with his cheap aftershave. The garlic and thyme were like smelling salts that revived her; she felt reborn, as though these were the beginnings of a new life as a truly cosmopolitan woman full of impetuous insouciance. She eased her coat off her shoulders.

"Kiss these," Adina said as she crossed her arms, taking up the bottom of her silk blouse and raising it over her black lace bra and over her head.

The quivering flesh burst through the thin fabric. Upturned cones and the deep, plunging groove between them. Hadid helped himself to the bra snap, conveniently in front.

For Hadid, this unveiling triggered much more than the kiss—the voluptuous contours of her high, firm breasts provocatively suspended her pointed nipples and fired impulses through his eyes to an indeterminate point in his brain. These pulses sent signals through his ganglia. His erection strained inside white jeans, longing for the almost certain liberation to come sooner rather than later.

For Adina, the sensation was the same in a different way. By exposing her sensitive white skin to this dark foreigner, she opened herself up to many new sensations—her entire being was charged with a vulnerable feeling of anticipation focused in her rosy nipples. The instant he touched them, the fibers radiating from the papillae rose up to greet his fingers, sending shock waves to her nerves, all over her body. Her tongue became dry, and as she parted her lips, her nose quivered, inhaling Hadid's scent; her ears burned as if all her blood ran there in expectation of some clue as to what she should do.

Without speaking, he pressed her breasts together with one hand from underneath and rubbed the rosy glands with the palm of his other hand. Adina had the desperate feeling they would pop. She gasped, threw back her head. Hadid heard it crack into the brick wall.

"Very well, take off your clothes and get ready for the shower." Hadid removed his hands.

Startled, Adina clutched her breasts. "What?"

"What? What do you mean, 'What?' Can't you hear the bodies being tortured upstairs? The bones breaking? Don't tell me you've never heard that line about a shower from the camps—we only do to you and your friends what they would do to us, what your grandparents did to the Jews."

Adina looked at him in disbelief. He nodded. "The gas chamber."

The faint stink of Turkish food permeated the air, filling her sensitive nose with disgust. She began to laugh. She laughed freely and deeply, like she'd never laughed before, and when she saw Hadid smile back at her it was as if she were floating on a magic carpet. Her reflexive, uncontrollable breaths made a sound she'd never heard before. She was laughing at the person she was an instant ago, at her ignorance and arrogance, her prissiness, which she now saw as ridiculous. Her ribcage was a prison for the feelings of freedom that escaped from her lungs, laughter triggered by the air of eucalyptus in a Turkish bath. A rope fell in spirals through the weak light as Adina wrapped her arms around Hadid's neck.

"You've reminded me how to laugh," she whispered.

His eyes shot up at the hole in the ceiling and then back to her. "You mean, you didn't know how?"

"No . . . I . . . There was always something holding me back. And when I think about what you said," she said, "I can't believe it. I was so stupid to take you seriously."

He caressed her breasts with expertise. "And you've taught me beauty."

Adina would have laughed at this, but she noticed a rope dangling next to her, twisting in the light as a young woman shimmied down it; a slinky blond in dirty white jeans and a black wool sweater. Hadid blinked, nodded for her to join them on the floor.

"We share everything here," she insisted. "Isn't that right, Hadid?"

Hadid nodded, lowering his eyes.

"I'm Anne."

Intimidated by this striking woman who so brazenly ruptured the intimate moment, intimidated by her piercing green eyes, Adina began to button her blouse.

"No, I don't want to stop you, I want to join you. You're very pretty and Hadid . . ." Her voice trailed off with the glance she threw his way.

They all laughed. In a supple motion, Anne pulled off her sweater. Strands of long blond hair crackled with static electricity. Hadid marveled at the two women, the realism of their four young breasts and the sensuality they expressed by the look in their eyes. He watched Anne take a small black bottle from her jeans pocket.

"Mutschler ink, from Heidelberg—the very best," Anne said as she extracted a long needle in a leather case. "Where do you want it?"

"What?"

Anne looked at Hadid.

"We didn't get that far," he said.

"Why not on your half shave?" Anne laughed a little. "If you're with us, you shave so everyone can see the @; if you're against us, well, you can just grow your hair and we'll have left our mark."

Adina was with them—anything to restore her endlessly elusive sense of community and belonging. For an instant she wondered what her mother, who hated the Nazi use of tattoos, would think, but then decided she didn't care.

She nodded at Anne, who beamed back. Setting her ink and implements on a piece of paper on the floor, Anne used candles to sterilize the needle near the end. Adina flinched at the first stab, then relished the prickly sensation. Anne was an artist and took her time.

"Let me," Anne whispered as she set down the needle, "show you mine."

She wiggled her white jeans over her hips and down to her knees with her breasts jiggling in fields of wheat-blonde hair.

Buried in a discreet corner of curly tendrils—naturally fair pussy moss—was the identifying sign inscribed in her skin. She leaned over Anne's lap to get a better look.

"How come you don't shave?" Adina asked.

"Oh, I do sometimes—when I have to, that is. Maybe you can tell; I'm not like most of the hardcore punkers around here."

"Yeah, you're an ecowhore," Hadid cut in, "like Mother Earth, you've been strip-mined, plowed and raped to near death. Yet, look at you; you're still beautiful, still willing to give man the sustenance he needs." Hadid made a philosophical wave. "Look at her, will you? These soft curves bruised from battle with faschos—her body is a metaphor for the planet." He ran his hand down her side. "The fertility goddess Demeter arrives by winged snake and finds her long-lost daughter Persephone in the underworld. Since we've sacrificed the pigs, let's delve deeper into the Eleusinian Mysteries in hope of a happy future full of poppies and pomegranates."

Adina had only a vague idea what Hadid was talking about. Pigs, poppies, pomegranates—these artificial symbols of fertility were truly a mystery to her. Nonetheless, the talk furthered her feeling that she had nothing to lose with them but her whips and chains.

Anne lifted herself a little and spread Adina's fur-trimmed leather coat on the floor, kicking her jeans all the way off. Adina did the same with her silk pants and panties. Hadid stood before the two women for an instant, then tore off his coat, shirt, boots and jeans.

Adina followed Anne's lead—up on their knees, with a hot breath on Hadid's half-hard staff. The head peeped out of its sheath. A warm hand . . . moist lips . . . more moist lips. Hadid was in heaven. He ran his hands through their blond and brunette hair, felt their hands clasp his bottom and nails rake his back. Adina and Anne each licked Hadid's length, alternating with each other kissing and sucking the knob. Anne made little slurping sounds as she kissed the head, licking with each kiss. Adina opened her mouth wider, sucked harder, as if she depended on drinking him.

Anne suddenly reversed herself and assumed a provocative position on all fours—her luscious ass in the air, her head buried in a pile of wheat-blond hair. Hadid immediately dropped to his knees, to the magnetic field. He parted the lips and followed the attraction of his iron shaft.

Anne knew well that a jaded fuck like Hadid liked the aesthetic aspect of oral sex but preferred the straight ahead genital variety best. Adina was left holding Hadid's balls, until she heard Anne softly call, "Adina, Adina."

"What do you want?" Adina asked, a trace of jealousy in her voice.

"I want you. Come, sit here." Anne patted the ground in front of her head. "Feed me your pussy."

Adina was surprised, both by the request and the obscene way it was expressed. She'd never experienced a woman. Feed me your cunt? Adina thought with disdain, yet the obscenity of the request brought on that overwhelming sensation that made her breasts flush and tingle.

Her back against the cold, grimy wall; her legs over Anne's shoulders . . . the sensations were beyond Adina's former realm of experience—an intense new language of love articulated itself in the feeling of tender female lips on her clit, of Anne's supple tongue darting across her prepuce and down her fouchette[27].

---

[27]    A thin fold of skin at the back of the vulva.

The woman sought out tender spots around the dark folds after thoroughly drenching the moss that adorned Adina's pudenda. Her teeth nibbled here and bit there, uncovering the quivering button of flesh that was engorged and upstanding. Adina shivered and spread her legs wider, her hands now on Anne's head, her fingers interlaced in Anne's hair. More pressure. Affirmative gasps. Anne looked up and smiled, Adina's juices glistening on her lips. She immediately returned to her task, lapping fervently and plunging as much tongue as deep as she could.

Hadid, meanwhile, wiggled Anne's voluptuous hips, pushed his thumb in her rectum along with a powerful stroke of cock in her willing cunt. Her breathing was shallow, lower than the smacking sound of Hadid's belly on her upturned buttocks. With his free hand, he reached under her belly and caressed the soft flesh. The three-part harmony he played with her ass, cunt and belly sounded a crescendo in Anne—she came in a series of convulsions whose diminishing intensity had the opposite effect on Adina and Hadid: the former looking down on Anne's head, buried between long Prussian legs, as female-tongue spoke urgently of orgasm to a hairless cunt; the latter's cock becoming the subject and object of Anne's convulsions—it compressed and expanded inside her cunt in muscular, semen-dripping spasms.

Adina beckoned Hadid with outstretched hands. He pulled out of Anne, who slumped to the dirty floor while continuing drinking honey from the hive. Hadid wrapped his hands around Adina's skull. His fingers wove into her moist brunette hair to protect her head from the wall. Adina's already open lips parted wider to accommodate Hadid's organ anointed with Anne's oil.

The Turk's belly pressed against Adina's forehead as he thrust inside her mouth. Adina began to squirm—Anne was still licking and Hadid's presence was too distracting for Adina to come. His pubes tickled her nose, his balls slapped her chin, his large uncircumcised head probed deeply in her throat.

Anne was too expert, too persistent to let Adina's squirming deter her tongue. In the darkness of the coal room, buried in her own thick blond hair and Adina's slippery tissues, Anne searched for her new friend's orgasm with the determination of Demeter in search of her daughter. A quiver, a convulsion . . . Adina's scream was muffled by Hadid's dick tattooing her throat. Garlic, thyme, sperm—Adina sucked Hadid's root with relish, drinking the last bit of his spunk. And when Hadid fell back on the coal bin, the seed goddesses kissed—they passed the milk back and forth with their lips and tongues and pussies.

# CHAPTER 14

❀

If one is knocked out in a bad dream, which is what Richard would've liked the battle with the autonomes to have been, one wakes up. His eyes opened slowly to this strange yet verifiable truth. Only it wasn't a dream, he thought in an instance where a blow to the head can make one more conscious, not less, of reality. Richard came to in the modern urban nightmare of a Berlin squat. The wreckage of the communal apartment, now truly communalized by the autonomes, surrounded him. He was chained and tied naked to his iron bed. Someone was between his legs.

"Where's Adina?" The effort to speak hurt Richard's battered head.

"She's getting her brains fucked out by a handsome Turk," Jutte said, grabbing a fistful of Richard's massive snake, "and loving it."

The near nausea of imagining his dear Adina with a dark foreigner was increased when Richard lifted his head and saw Jutte: the fleshy folds, the lip ring, WORK, NO THANKS tattooed on her forehead. Richard's head fell back on the bed and he closed his eyes.

But his mighty staff had a mind of its own under the persuasive influence of lonely Jutte, even with her lip ring partially in the way of complete oral pleasure. Richard didn't dare open his eyes to see her moving over him and her flesh settling over his pole.

"I don't think I've ever wanted to be fucked by the state before," Jutte said with heavy sarcasm as she lowered more of her weight onto his rod.

The iron bed creaked. Richard pulled on the chains and rope, testing his bonds. Tears welled in his eyes.

"Oh, you're no martyr," Jutte said. "Do your duty. Stab me."

Jutte's personal history, as she saw it, was a losing war with the state—so this was a rare opportunity to actually fuck the state. He felt the sticky sweat from her bush on his stomach; their smegma collected on him and clung to her lips, except below where her juices drained down his balls. She humped on him furiously with her sopping pussy, bouncing on the polystyrene mattress with her knees. Richard again strained against the chains, his veins and muscles bulging, a worried look on his face.

Jutte rocked back and forth, milking his cock with her overgrown pussy lips. Despite her appearance, she was tight, and with a shiver of revulsion Richard felt himself responding. His cock thickened and lengthened. She took everything he gave and shifted down on him for more, rolling her hips forward, her thick fingers resting on his muscled chest then roving over her own flopping breasts. Up and down. She drove the breath from him with each downstroke. He was close to erupting, but Jutte beat him to it and came with a whimper.

So how long has it been for her? Richard thought, flexing his big prick in frustration as she eased off him.

She threw a sack dress over her rotund body and left the room. A moment later, three punks emerged and freed Richard from the bed—at gunpoint. The kid with the revolver looked familiar, but Richard couldn't place him.

"Why don't we let him have it?" The kid cocked the gun. "That way, he will never come back. You can see how he is—he thinks he owns the world."

The voice, the long hair, the insolence—Richard remembered now; he was the kid who lived in the building before the wall came down. He was probably the one who led the autonomes here. What had he said about Adina? Richard wondered as he pulled on his pants. Something about pollution . . . Rostock?

"Let's just get him the fuck out of here," Mohawk rasped. "Hurry up, old man. If it takes you longer than it would take us to clean up your blood, you're through."

Richard stuffed his feet into his shoes and stumbled toward the door, held open by a redskin.

"Let me escort you out," the kid with the gun began, "even though you know the way."

They filed downstairs. Richard felt faint, steadied himself on the banister.

"Keep going." The kid waved the gun. "Who's laughing now, old man?"

They traversed the now clear entranceway toward the hastily repaired doorway. Mohawk opened the door.

"Get out! And don't come back," the kid who'd lived there shouted, shoving Richard into the early evening rain.

A cold wind whipped through the streets as Richard zipped up his jacket, snagging a tuft of chest hair. A sucker punch hit him—from an orange-haired passerby. Punch drunk, he stumbled through the fog that wafted into a mercury sky. The dull shimmer of headlights on wet cobblestone blocks.

"Taxi!"

As Richard turned, the blurred brakelights' diffused reflection on the moist asphalt cast on his face and lit up a cracked first floor window. If there were any beauty left to Berlin, Richard thought, it was in these chance superimpositions of light and darkness, man and machine. He climbed into a cab to begin a fragmented taxi ride through the maze of streets.

*

The taxi pulled to a stop in front of the Free Ring.

"Shit. My wallet, they took my wallet," Richard said to the taxi driver, who looked worried. "Don't worry," Richard went on. "I'll be right back."

He pulled himself out of the car, disappointed his Stasi seal no longer paid his way and twitching with pains in his neck and ribs to go with his throbbing head. Heads turned as Richard pushed through the bar door.

"What happened to you?" the barman asked. "Get in a cat fight?"

"Yeah, yeah," Richard said as he made for the back room.

"Anya, would you cover my cab outside?"

"Sure, Richard. Are you alright?"

"No, I'm not. Alright?" Richard slumped in her chair as she left to pay the cab, sitting with an assembly of sex workers without customers. "I'm glad to see you're all working."

A thin-faced sex worker named Inseln dipped her napkin in a glass of water and dabbed his head as she spoke. "The few customers we've had were stuck on a new woman—she's a knockout. What happened to you?"

"I don't want to talk about it," Richard said quietly.

The thought of a new woman took his mind off his injuries and helped reverse the revulsion he'd experienced at the hands of the anarchist. Strangely, the only images he could conjure of the new women weren't of Anya, who had been quite new, not so long ago, but of Adina—first as he'd last seen her, then as he remembered her from her westie boyfriend's video.

"Where's this new one?" Richard asked.

"She's working." Anya nodded toward the door. "The customers have been pleased."

Richard stood up; a woman grabbed him.

"Hey, easy with my hand. I want to try her."

Another sex worker, Patricia, looked up from her place at the table. "Are you sure you're up for it?"

"Doesn't it look like I deserve a little pleasure after all the pleasure I go through for you?"

At that moment, the john waltzed out of the room. "She's lovely," he said, "simply lovely."

"Say, you in there," Patricia yelled. "You got another fuck in those young bones of yours?"

"Why not?" a sweet voice called out through the wall to the restaurant.

"Get ready for a big one then," Patricia said loudly, then more quietly: "It's on me, Richard. Just wear one of these. We found some extra large condoms just for guys like you."

She slid a square packet down the table. Richard grumbled something as he picked up the condom, then stepped into the pitch-black room. He left off the light, wanting to feel the new woman's freshness while Adina's erotic video played in his mind.

The room smelled of sex, or, to be more specific, it smelled of cunt—light, fresh, young cunt. She knew what was expected of her; indeed, she was hot for a big one . . . one last long fuck at the end of her first day at her new job. Even if he was bit smelly himself, her bitch-in-heat scent overpowered everything.

That sultry feminine odor, combined with the images of Adina stretching for the camera in a swim cap—her protuberant tits and ass, her hairless cunt. Richard hardened as he stripped in the shadows. He fumbled with the condom, tearing the foil with his oversized fingers.

The wrapper fell to the floor and he rolled the slippery rubber over his organ. Kneeling on the bed between her legs, Richard watched Adina in his mind's video screen take the first crack at Albert with the rubber hose. Richard rubbed the rubber in the new woman's juicy folds, imagining Adina's labia traced with lipstick. He fell in her.

"You'll earn your pay with me," Richard whispered as he began his thrusts that mimicked the movements of Bronson fighting in the background of a video Adina had made with her westie boyfriend: the slow motion intercut of the bad actor's facial scars, his deadpan stare at a fresh corpse.

The new woman's yelps echoed in the empty room as he fucked her forcefully, as the others must have given the slack he felt in her organ. As Richard imagined Adina sinking her ass over Albert's face, Richard's vision was likewise blank, or better said, black in the dark room. Dick's little white death spurted from his eponymous body part that was the center of so much of his violence against women, and the condom's spermicide shot searing pain down his shaft to his balls, bitter medicine for the man of bitter passion. He bit into her left tit. She screamed passionately while feeling for the lamp, then she flipped on the switch. The rookie sex worker saw the top of his head as he kissed the breast to make it better. He looked up in the light and instantly realized his savage fear between the legs of his daughter, his own flesh and blood. She too was shocked and pushed at his hairy chest…to get away from him.

\*

Jan knew from experience and his Reichian sexpol studies that he could now do with Charlotte whatever he wanted—she was with him, not somewhere else as sometimes happens with whores. She was with him and submitting to his desires. He straddled her and ran the tip of his pole over her nipples. She crooked her neck and opened her mouth again. Jan lifted the lowest chain that ran from one shoulder pad to the other with his cock in an arch that rose and fell over her mountainous breasts. The smooth skin on the head of his cock brushed her cheek and she turned to again catch it and the chain cutting across his rod…to catch them with her lips and tongue, tying his thick cock in mail and grazing her teeth over the flesh and metal. Jan lurched forward, pushing into her face and tightening the tension on his tool. She drooled on him with hungry lips as the chain loosened and spiraled off his now naked stand.

Both Jan and Charlotte were unable to put a face on the next voice on the screen—they were too preoccupied: "At first, it was hard to accept a long series of sexual acts that I considered immoral. Now I think it's immoral to think of sex as immoral. What gets me are the hypocrites who try to justify why they come. Most guys think prostitutes are idiots and they're intent on telling us about adventures they've had with women they've only dreamed of. Then there are those who ask, 'What's a nice young woman like you doing in a place like this?' I can't stand those—they like to think that they're better than we are."

At the mention of immoral acts, Jan unhooked his cock and turned around, clambering on his knees. He faced the camera with his feet pressed against Charlotte's shoulder pads. He straightened his glasses and stroked his cock with his right hand, slowly lowering his muscular buns onto Charlotte's pretty face. He felt her hands on his ass, opening the cleft.

I hope she doesn't find any crab eggs under my scrotum, he thought. What'll her husband think when he sees this? Rim jobs can't be on her regular menu.

"Yes," he gritted through clenched teeth as her tongue eased into his rectum.

Jan watched Albert raise his finger to his mouth to signal for quiet as the next woman appeared on the screen. A large woman smiled at the camera, and as she shifted, the eye of the camera filled with massive breasts tied together by a black elastic ribbon, giving her boobs the aspect of balloons.

The interviewee's words fell on his ears but Jan didn't hear what she was saying. His hips waved on Charlotte's nose and then backed away. The sensation was too intense. He turned and traced a line with his cock down her neck and then between her chain-covered groove and down a bit further, he pushed into her plush belly with his rod. Nibbling one pastie-tipped nipple, then the other one—she groaned at his bites, turned her head away and pushed him off her breasts. Be that way, you beautiful ass-licking bitch, he thought, let's just get it on. He stood on his knees and peeled the tight-fitting condom over his girth, hooked the crooks of his elbows behind the back of her knees and positioned himself at the gateway to heaven. He thrust inside.

Charlotte's lips gasped in response to his thrusts. Jan watched her breasts jiggle in the mirrors on the closet door. All I want is to come-to-be, he thought, which is what the director wants, although he wouldn't put it that way. Jan hadn't mastered his sensuality, but he was a sensual master who could come-to-be on command. He summoned images of young women on the nude beaches of Holland and France bending over for seashells to show the passerby their nether parts— the images propelled him to greater velocity. He gave her hip thrusts and greedy squeezes, watching her hot breasts sway in the mirrors on the closet door.

Suddenly something made Jan want to lash out at her image as reflected in the mirror. It was probably a social-trigger cocked by images of archetypal beauties on the beach and stereotyped reactions to them—not by the lively flesh and blood in hand with whom he'd waged such a glorious simulation of seduction but a two-dimensional image in his mind. He knew better, he couldn't help himself. It was something deep that came from the formation of his mind or from…from he didn't know where. The whore on the screen was having her final say.

"It doesn't matter. Today, all that matters is that I feel good, and in order to do that I have to live by fucking imbeciles. Drunks? They're everywhere, but they're not the only idiots."

Jan slapped the side of Charlotte's ass with the cup of his hand and her white skin flushed red; once, thrusting—twice, thrusting harder—three times, erupting in spurts in, and still deeper into, her satiny slit.

"The only thing that really counts for me in my life," the sex worker said on the video, "is fucking like animals."

"That's a take," Albert said.

Jan pumped the last drops of come out of his snake, milking the free fuck with her strong cunt for a last scrap of pleasure. He fell back on the bed with a low groan.

Charlotte looked over her shoulder with a smile. "I'm glad you liked it."

Jan closed his eyes.

# CHAPTER 15

The brief warm spell broke like a bone under a fascho boot the day Jan returned to the State Hotel for a final shot. He was due to get paid, although he had doubts about what he would accept. He marched through cold, moist air with thoughts of a Serner story about a woman with dilated pupils from belladonna and features that were deformed by pleasure. What, Jan wondered, would the author do in my shoes? Probably try to sell a manifesto to a rich friend and move on to the next city. Somewhere warmer than Berlin, ideally Paris, where obscene literature was celebrated.

If Serner had kept moving, the Nazis might not have been able to track him. It was hard for Jan to imagine his hero, who had changed his lodgings the way others changed underwear, settling down and teaching in a school. Did this avowed con artist eventually feel so morally bound to his wife and students that he grew clay feet? "If you want to sleep with me," Serner wrote, "you must ask me more clearly." This was a line that could be used at choice moments and likely obtain the desired result, unlike so much of literature, which Jan reminded himself was useless crap.

He pushed through the front door to the hotel, nodding to coworkers. Crossing the lobby, his cold fingers unbuttoned his wool coat. He took a deep breath as the elevator doors opened. Jan could almost imagine making a few shrewd moves, fleecing the movie director he was working for and taking his costar with him to Paris—something akin to the shrewdness in Serner's philosophy that found truth in deceit, which Jan admired but didn't accept because it induced sadness. There are principles to live by beyond simply obtaining what one wants, Jan thought as he walked down the hall and approached the door. He knocked; the door opened.

"Hello," Albert said.

Jan nodded hello, still thinking about the dada philosopher's dictums against having a fixed identity—the way, for example, he easily gave up writing and the role of being a writer—as well as his harangues against idealism.

"The star," Albert said gesturing toward Charlotte, "has been here for quite some time."

Jan stepped into the room and found Charlotte with the black collar around her neck—her only garment. He pictured her on her belly and then on all fours like a dog, the bob of hair on her head bouncing up and down. Good to see you again, he thought, let's get your big breasts moving for the camera.

Albert took aim. "Action."

Jan's hand ran around her back and clamped her waist, leaning in for an alcoholic kiss. She didn't mind his breath or touch; she reached for his cock. Her pussy quivered as her hand brushed over his prick, through his trousers. He took off his shirt. She let him back up and kick off his shoes and slip off his pants.

The camera was rolling, but only now, nude, did Jan look directly at it and slowly peel on a condom. The touch on his shoulder—her hand, her hair. He turned, pressed his cock into her belly, cradling her ass as he shuttled her against the wall. She writhed against him. The silhouette formed of Jan easing into her standing up, raising her right leg up, pressing against her slim belly. Scudding thoughts came to Jan of the other whores Albert had interviewed on television as he plunged in and farther into Charlotte's widespread legs with powerful strokes. Jan suddenly turned, pivoted with her in his arms and fell on the bed. He pinioned her on the mattress with a slight wobble of the bed as his surges instantly recommenced.

Her fluffy blond hair formed a fan over the side of the bed. Bundles of it tumbled over the edge like straw over the rails of a truck bouncing down a dirt road. A woman with the most sensitive face yet appeared on the screen. She had keen brown eyes, a narrow nose with delightful arches at her nostrils, a fine jaw line, brunette hair accented with a silk rose behind her ear. Her bright red lips and cheeks matched the red beads around her neck. Her voice cracked sweetly as if it were hard for her to have her say.

"My name is Kirsten," she said. "After the wall, I tried to live in the west with my mother, but I didn't know anyone and everyone seemed so cold. When I came back, I couldn't find my father. One thing led to another. An old friend was working out of the Free Ring, a little bar near Oranienburger Tor. I really enjoyed my first day—until my father found me."

Jan held himself up with one arm and Charlotte by the beginning of the curve between her narrow waist and molded hips with the other, then moving to her breasts, holding both at once. He began clockwise gyrating thrusts, rotating her tits counter-clockwise. No sensation of moisture with the condom on, just tightness and heat amid the sounds of love and her scent. He bent her legs back and licked her slender calves while listening to Kirsten tell her tale.

"I can imagine what you're thinking: her father saw her go into that bar and went in and nabbed her. It wasn't like that at all. My father was Stasi, and after the wall came down, he was out of work and became a pimp. Oh, he probably still killed people, but he didn't get paid for it anymore. If you could see my father, you would understand—he's a monster. I'd been with a bunch of men that day, when one of the other women called: 'Hey, you got another fuck in those young bones of yours?'"

"'Why not?' I said

"'Get ready for a big one.'

"In all truth, I remember thinking: A nice big one at the end of the day? I'm going to like this job."

What the hell is she talking about? Jan asked himself. He felt Charlotte's calves scissor around his neck. Jan looked down on her lips as a perverse smile spread across them.

Kirsten wiped a tear from her eye and the ruby red nail polish flashed across the screen. "I heard him undress in the dark—it surprised me because all the other men wanted to look at me. He knelt on the bed, then fell on me. 'You'll earn your pay with me,' he said."

Charlotte tightened her grip on Jan's head with her calves, squeezing his temples until his face turned red. His glasses were askew, his hair no longer stuck out—it fell to his scalp from the sweat. Charlotte tightened her grip, tensing her ass and thighs—her cunt closed around him.

"I hate remarks like that." Kirsten shook her head for the camera. "What a thing to say. My pussy was already a little sore and it seemed as if he wanted to hurt me more."

Jan thrust into Charlotte with the force of his muscular back. He sensed the rubber was in shreds—too much stress on the thin latex sheath. Charlotte's moisture and pressure engulfed his senses. He gasped for air. She looks like a gladiator with those shoulder pads and knives in her ears. If she has her way, I won't be long for this world. Never more will I come-to-be, Jan thought as he leaned into his last thrust before orgasm.

Kirsten's words on the video shattered any hope of postcoital bliss: "I was crying for help, but nobody came. He was biting my tit when he finished. By then I was screaming, trying to turn on the light. Finally, I found it. And when I turned it on, I found my father all right."

Charlotte loosened her grip on Jan's neck as he pumped the last spurts inside her with feelings of pleasure and relief battling with empathy for Kirsten and regret that the condom had broken. He eased out, pulled off the remains, the straining rubber ring at the base of his shaft, so she wouldn't know what had happened. He gently lay over her and kissed her breasts.

What do I have to lose, he asked himself as he worked his way down and massaged her hairy mount with the flat of his tongue. Her husband must eat it—a woman like this wouldn't be married to a fool. It must be safe. He darted his tongue across her clit, backed off to cool her pussy with his breath and glimpse the pool of sperm dripping out her laceration, as the French theorists thought of vaginas. The images Kirsten painted in the video reminded him of other tales of incest and abuse he'd heard on his way up in life—they made him feel guilty to be a man. He wanted to confess to crimes he'd never committed. He thought of the unromantic love he had for so many people and things, of a dog playing with a bright yellow ball, and those images touched off the memory of tales told by a lover—how her twenty-year-old brother tricked her eighteen-year-old sister while in a wooded park on the outskirts of Warsaw. In what would point to the inevitability of justice prevailing—if it didn't indicate the greater abuse of women by men—the brother grew up to marry one of the richest women in Poland, only she came with a big catch. It turned out his wife had also been abused and was now a psychiatric basket case he had to live with.

Abuse . . . abuse . . . echoed in Jan's skull as Charlotte trembled and moaned in orgasm. As a Pole, it was impossible for him to live without morals and good will. It's so easy to make them happy—why don't all men treat women this way? Jan asked himself. As if returning the gift, Charlotte hoisted her leg over his head and positioned herself on all fours. They were oblivious to Albert, who was still shooting. Jan was half hard from licking her—her orgasm and the sight of her open lips, blond muff and plush, velvet-smooth ass stiffened him up enough to get back inside.

On each stroke her luscious ass compressed with his weight, then snapped back instantly, again attaining its perfect shape. Her back muscles rippled under the swaying chains and tufts of fluffy hair. She reminded him now of the Czech women who wore tight miniskirts, but no underwear, walking in the park or sunning themselves without caring who saw. The memory made him come-to-be again.

"Cut. That's a wrap." Albert moved in front of the camera. "You were excellent, Johann. As for you, Charlotte, a stellar performance. I'll have to give you both a little extra—"

"Money?" Jan cut in, opening his eyes. "I don't want it; don't pay me at all, not to experience her—that's an end in itself."

Charlotte smiled, leaned back and lit a cigarette. "At least take this."

She threw a silver-plated lighter to him.

"Thank you sincerely, Charlotte, I will treasure this," he said while examining the trademark 'S.T. Dupont – PARIS' etched into the metal. "Other than this, all I'd like is a little food and drink." He emphasized the last word.

"What's your poison?"

"Vodka, no, make it whiskey and beer—the way they drink in Hollywood."

They were dressing—Charlotte wrapped in a black lace shawl—as the bellboy wheeled in a room service cart laden with food. He nodded toward Jan but couldn't keep his eyes off Charlotte.

"Where's the booze?" Jan asked.

The bellboy pulled back the tablecloth, revealing a shelf of bottles: champagne, beer, whiskey and vodka.

"Great," Jan said to the bellboy as he buttoned his shirt. "Now if you don't mind."

The bellboy left, looking back at Charlotte as he closed the door behind himself. The director popped the champagne and poured glasses for Charlotte and himself, then passed Jan a beer.

"To the oldest profession in the world," Albert said.

"To Charlotte," Jan proposed.

She smiled over the rim of her champagne flute, pleased with herself and happy with the way it had worked out. She leaned back in her chair and took out another cigarette.

Jan set his beer bottle on the coffee table and looked Albert in the eye. "You should do something with Kirsten's interview—I couldn't believe my ears."

"Who?" Albert took a sip. "You probably mean the one who was taken by her ex-Stasi father. What should I do about it?"

"I don't know," Jan said. "Take it to the authorities and see if they can make a case against him. If you put him behind bars, you'd be a hero. A guest once told me they have shows like that in America. The cops catch a crook and everyone sees how they do it. He said they love it."

Albert hummed in vague agreement, his mouth full of effervescent wine.

# CHAPTER 16

❁

A few weeks after his porn star debut, Jan spent the day—his day off—riding the U-bahn to escape the heat of Hell. They'd managed to fix the water and the furnace roared next to his room. He felt cramped working with the pipes hanging from the low ceiling above his writing desk as if there weren't space in the room for his thoughts. The place simmered. So instead of staying in, he played Cortázar's Parisian women-watching game in the Berlin subway windows—trying to think of himself more as an actor than a writer. A nice one looked away when he met her eyes with his.

Spandau, Zitadelle, Haselhorst—it was already late afternoon when the train pulled into Deutsche Oper. A familiar person appeared on the platform, ready to get in the train.

Jan sidestepped in front of the man and smiled. "Herr Director."

"Oh, it's you," Albert said.

Jan turned, allowing the director to board, slapping him on the shoulder. The men shuffled down the aisle and grabbed handrails above their heads as the train lurched forward.

"How have you been?" Albert asked.

"I could be better. Say, I wanted to congratulate you on your coup. From what I heard, your piece on the ex-Stasi pimp and his sex worker daughter was excellent."

"Yes, looking back on it, I owe you for your suggestion that I track down this Richard Wurzer character." Albert reached for his wallet.

Jan held up his hand. "These are not the things for which one takes money."

"Please," Albert said.

"I simply won't take your money." Jan shook his head. "Just tell me how you found him."

"It was easy," Albert said. "I started with those people, you know, the ones who're after the old party bosses. They led me to sources in the united German government's clearinghouse for Stasi records, who launched the investigation."

"Bravo," Jan said.

"You saw the show?" Albert asked.

"No." Jan hesitated, about to say that he never watched television. "I read about it."

"You were smashing. It's only a shame that we had to air it so late at night, but then again, you don't want children watching you and Charlotte."

Jan nodded. "What're you working on now?"

"A few odds and ends, no big projects in the works."

"You know, I'm living in the squats near Samariterstrasse. I don't know if I can help much, but you might think about doing something with what's going on over there."

"What do you have in mind?"

"You're the director. All I know is that we get reporters from all over the world prowling around. After the city raided the area and we successfully defended the squat—there are even more journalists now. It's become a pretty hot issue. You should check it out. I can take you there."

"I'm always on the lookout for new images," Albert said.

Jan pointed the case Albert had in hand. "What's that? You have your camera?"

Albert nodded as the train pulled to a stop at Charlottenburg station.

"This station always reminds me of Charlotte's beauty," Jan said as they changed trains.

Albert nodded. "I enjoyed her too."

Jan ignored the implication of Albert's remark. "Should we change again at Marx-Engels Platz and try to find her on the streets near Oranienburger Tor or at the Free Ring?"

"No." Albert turned away. "I don't think I'd better show up over there with so many of Richard's friends around."

"You worry too much," Jan laughed. "Those guys are running for their lives." Jan reached in his bag for another bag, the one with the bottle. "Have a drink?"

"Don't mind if I do," Albert said.

"Help yourself, this time it's on me." Jan handed him the bag.

Albert inspected the bottle. "Hmm, Polish. Good stuff."

"You know, Albert, there's a few things we ought to get straight if we're going to be drinking buddies."

Albert's eyebrows rose.

"First of all, my name is Jan and I'm Polish—you have a problem with that?"

"No, why should—"

"Never mind. Second, I have to tell you that I had a few problems with the show. I know it worked out that you helped catch that guy, but you did it for the money—admit it."

"Sure. You—" Albert wanted to accuse Jan of the same thing, but remembered he'd refused pay. "You originally wanted to do it for the same reason."

"I wasn't in my right mind, but I came to my senses. Now that the wall is down, the industrialists are back. And guess what? So are the prostitutes, in droves. The whores know the score. But from what I heard, you didn't draw the connection."

"You're telling me how to do my job," Albert said.

"I'm sorry, Albert. It's a sensitive point for me since I'm associated with the project. I always have to wonder if people recognize me. You know, I once submitted to an order by some of these Stasis to fuck a woman in the ass. You may meet her, she lives in the squats. I can't bring myself to speak with her now. With you, it was as if I was submitting to your ideology."

"Ideology? I don't have an ideology. I'm the least—"

"Albert, you have an ideology whether you know it or not. With you, the ideology of visibility is like a disease, this search for images of yours. It's the same ideology that propels the German entertainment industry."

Albert took another pull on the bottle. "You should be in the business—you certainly have lots of ideas."

"Albert." Jan took the bottle and wiped it with his sleeve— he grabbed the overhead handrail before drinking. "I'm a writer—of course I have ideas. What would you directors do without us? You need a few ideas, what do you do? You look on a bookshelf."

"What sort of writing do you do?"

"It doesn't matter." Jan took another swig. "All I can say is that I'll never be able to do what you do."

"Why take me to the squats?"

"Because we live philosophically there." Jan looked out the window for the right words. "And it could be that you can make good publicity in our battle of perception with the civic authorities. Awful ring to the phrase, don't you think? Civic authorities. It'll certainly test your powers of persuasion to get her to go along with the project—that is if you still want to do it."

"I want to do it—check it out, at least. But really, I want to know, what do you write?"

"Albert, you probably have no idea about anything worthwhile that has happened in the art world in the last forty years."

"You know, I do a little painting myself."

"Whatever you do, don't tell anyone in the squats about it. They'll put you on a stage and have you paint in public so they can ridicule you. That's the way it is. Let's go. This is our stop."

Above ground, Jan tossed the empty bottle in a trashcan and led Albert a few turns to the door of Hell. As they passed into the entrance alcove, the sleeping guard awoke, then closed his eyes again. At the end of the hall, Jan led Albert down a flight of stairs, through a metal fire door.

"So this is where I'm staying," Jan said.

"You live here?" Albert looked incredulously at the tangle of pipes hanging over Jan's straw bed, the desk held together with clamps.

"Temporary arrangement," Jan said. "I'll be on my way to Paris if things work out."

Pipes swayed with the weight of flowing water. They heard voices of guys stoking the furnace next door—the sound of shovels. Jan set his briefcase inside his room, turned and pushed through the heavy fire door.

"Go ahead." Jan held the door.

Albert climbed the stairs, and when he made the top stair, he bumped into the American women.

The black woman looked beyond the film director. "Hey, Jan, who is this?"

"Remember that show I was in?"

She nodded.

"Well, this is the director who made it," Jan said.

As Albert exchanged names and small talk with the Americans, Jan held up his hand for Albert to wait. Jan ran out the door, across the cobblestone street. In the likely event that his plans didn't work out—that he never made it to Paris—Jan had made friends with some of the people in the Alter Native: if a room opened up, he wanted it. He lit a cigarette—knocked.

"Who's there?"

Jan inscribed his name in the early evening shadows of the entrance with his lit smoke in case the guard was looking through the cracks in the door. Mohawk opened the door.

"Is Jutte around?" Jan asked.

"She's upstairs cooking."

Jan bound upstairs, following the smell of garlic and other spices. Nearing the kitchen, he overheard a guy pontificating.

"So I went into the alley to take a piss and there was this rat standing on his hind legs, holding his dick. I said, 'What's up?' as I started to go. I really had to go. When I looked back down, I noticed that his cock was bigger than mine."

"That reminds me of the time I electrocuted myself by pissing on an electric fence in the country."

"Will you guys quit talking about your dicks," Jutte said.

Jan stepped into the kitchen as Jutte was fishing orange peels out of a cast iron skillet in the porcelain sink. The guys were ripping into an uncut loaf of rye and dipping it in the juice of tomato and cucumber salad. Cans of beer stood on the table. Jaco Pastorius was on the boombox. Jan nodded hello and walked to the sink, doused his cig. He tossed it in the trash, on top of orange peels.

"When will you quit smoking, Jan?" Jutte asked.

"As soon as I quit writing. That smells great. I'm sorry to bother you, it's just that I've got this guy over in Hell who wants to do a show on the way we live—it might be good propaganda."

"I don't know," Jutte said. "I've just about had my fill of reporters."

"I remember you saying that was what we needed some good publicity. I'm friends with this guy so we could probably get him to film what we want."

"He's all right?"

"Sure." Jan stared at her blankly through his Brecht glasses.

"Here you go, guys." She pushed the meal out of the pan onto two plates. "It's all for you. I don't need to eat, I have to watch my figure."

Their mouths were too full to give thanks, but Jutte knew that they were thankful—appreciative that they had a surrogate mother who would take care of them. Jan motioned with his hand to lead her to the filmmaker.

"Who is he?" Jutte asked as she and Jan negotiated the stairs.

"His name's Albert."

They went out onto the sidewalk, then through a line of parked cars and crossed the street as a solitary man, a pipe between his teeth, crossed the cobblestones in the opposite direction. A car's jerky headlights headed for the philosopher on his walk.

"He makes films," Jan said.

Jutte arched her right eyebrow. "What sort of films?"

"You can ask him. He made a good sex worker documentary—that much I know. A television film. He also said that he makes those erotic videos he exchanges with members of a club, but that's just a hobby."

"That I'd like to see," Jutte said.

"Sounds like a bunch of amateurs getting their rocks off if you ask me." Jan looked ahead. "There he is."

Albert was waiting outside Hell with the American expatriates—despite their beauty, he was struck by the sight of Jutte as she approached: her WORK, NO THANKS tattoo, her BLUEPRINTS FOR MADNESS tee shirt. She looked like an interesting case.

"Well," Jan began, "since I've told each of you about the other, I can spare the introduction. You're in good hands, Albert. Now if you'll excuse me, I have some work of my own to do."

"Wait," Albert said.

Jan slapped Albert's left shoulder, then put his arms around the American women and walked them inside the squat. Jan was a chivalrous Pole who knew his role in leading the beauties away.

"So you're part of the military-industrial-entertainment complex," Jutte said.

"The what? I'm just a film director, sometimes a producer."

"You don't know what you are and you've probably never had a nonspectacular fuck in your life."

Looking at her in the halo of a streetlamp, he wondered what she meant by a nonspectacular fuck?

Jutte pointed at him accusingly. "You don't have the slightest idea what I'm talking about, do you?"

He glanced away.

"I can see it in your eyes," she said. "You have the same abnormal need for representation as the rest. It's your only compensation for the feeling of being on the margin of existence."

She was no longer attracted to the tall, curly haired director and recognized him as one of those objectifiers of women, a marketer of a fascist, packaged concept of beauty.

"For you," she went on, "the universe is as flat as a television screen, filled with fictional characters who surround you with their merchandise."

Jutte's impassioned rhetoric intrigued him—she was indeed a special case. He wished he'd been able to get her speech on film so he could watch it and listen to it over and over.

"You want," she continued, "to exist in a mirror image of the world rather than recognizing your own reality."

At least he was able to comprehend her aversion to film with her so clearly denigrating his profession in a way that made him defenseless.

"Come with me," she said.

They stepped into Jutte's room at the Alter Native with Albert gingerly following her, his camera in hand. The last remnants of a setting sun flooded her cozy yellow space. Batik throw pillows and a futon on the hardwood floor. Red satin sheets shimmering in the light. Jutte shut one blind, moved across the room, shut the other.

Albert stood just inside the door. "I won't be able to film in such low light."

"Who said we are making a film?" she asked while lifting her foot behind her, reaching down and taking a shoe off.

He nevertheless pushed record and filmed her with his camera eye as she repeated the gesture with the other shoe, observing how her pendulous breasts fell to one side.

"Lose the camera and get naked," she said.

A stiff breeze pushed through a crack in a broken window and the blind ruffled, sending a wave of light across the wall. While balancing on one foot, Albert pulled on his shoe, hopped, and wrenched it off. He watched Jutte unroll her leggings and take off her tee shirt. Her round, white body gleamed as she settled back in her red bed. Albert pushed off the second shoe, then dropped his trousers and drawers.

"Good, now get over here, Mr. Cameraman."

Her boobs jiggled as she motioned for him to come to her as if he were a dog; her dark bush glistened with moisture in the low light as she drew up her legs.

"You want to make a little movie of me?" Jutte asked. "Jan said you make erotic videos for a club of some sort. I'll give you and your friends a flick they'll never forget, but you have to let me do it my way."

"Your way is the only way," Albert said.

Albert shivered—unaccustomed to the chronic cold in squats—then he stepped toward her bed. Jutte loved the look of the nude man in her room and took in the sight with a beguiling smile. As he neared, she gripped his forearm and pulled him onto her ample, soft body. Ever since she'd had her way with Richard, her anarchist attitudes against domination disappeared in bed, where desire ruled.

"Watch this," she hissed as she pushed his head between her fleshy thighs. "Watch my pussy pulse."

Albert observed her overgrown labia, so slick with nectar, then he closed his eyes and allowed the scent alone to register in his brain, stirring his cock from shock-imposed slumber: the shocking sight of such long labia that now felt to his lips like kissing two tongues at once. Her fingers snake-danced through his curly blond hair as he slurped.

"This is better than video, isn't it?"

He said something but she muffled his reply by stretching his neck back and pulling his head into her. He bridled against her hand, resisting the long lips grinding against his, for an instant before succumbing to the tingling sensation. He puckered, licked, then puckered again as he sucked her slippery wet tissues between his teeth. His tongue searched out her clit and found it as she spread her legs wider. The sound of flesh scraping the crusty red sheet. She tickled his nose with her pubes as it rummaged around her mons. Her butt lifted up and banged on the bed. She twitched, trembled and tensed in orgasm. He sneezed.

The sneeze unglued her lips from his. She seized the opportunity to raise herself and crawl along the edge of the bed. Albert turned, watching with fascination how smoothly she moved. She pushed him in the same direction as he turned, pushed him on his back and straddled his hips. His eyes roved from her forehead tattoo down to her breasts. She climbed on her knees up to his neck. He strained as the hanging lips were about to engulf his mouth.

"Wait," he said.

"What for?"

He pushed his slender frame back under her, back so his shaft aimed into her slot. She sank over him, hunching and undulating, pulling his cock in and in, lurching deeper with little movements that flashed fear through his mind. Big woman, tight cunt, he thought. His shaft sluiced into her with each lurch. He opened his eyes to see her jaws flash past his face and feel her teeth sink into his neck. She rode his reed hard with her carnivorous flower, nurtured as it was in the hothouse of anarchist decadence, blossoming in jagged red petals that contrasted so vibrantly with her black pubes and white thighs.

"Tell me this Mr. Cameraman," she said while conjuring images of fucking the camera's eye and the society that watched while drowning in self-made pools of toxic waste, "isn't this better than a video?"

"You're so passionate," Albert said. "Don't stop."

# CHAPTER 17

If Albert had been able—both bodily (he was too exhausted to stop servicing Jutte) and mentally (he was drawn to her powerful denigration of his identity)—to leave Jutte's room and film the squats in the crackling light of dawn, he could have caught young people loving seditiously. Jutte's matronly charms and his instinctive side-to-side rolling like a swimmer in surging waves, waves foaming at their crests from a blue wind, deprived him and his audience their cinematic inspection beginning with Adina resting in bed in the next room.

She didn't hear the well-oiled door open, but a slight draft brushed her naked back sending shivers up her spine. Goosebumps flourished on Adina's sensitive skin and the fine hairs stood on end from a scent that filled the room, Hadid. Her nostrils quivered, otherwise she was still, resting nude on a scrap of carpet. Her eyes were riveted to an indeterminate point outside the panes she had just scraped with a razor and washed with dishwashing liquid.

A transparent window without distortion on a powder-blue sky. Low clouds drifted by, the sun rays that bathed her body dimmed slightly, yet illuminated the gray creases in the clouds that took on the aspect of a giant brain. Adina propped her elbow on a pillow on the floor, held her head in her hand—on the shaved side, near her now not-so-new tattoo.

As he approached, she slid her right foot along the carpet to her left knee, forming a triangle with her legs. One point of the triangle was itself a triangle, her warm pussy. She arched her back and her swollen rump pressed against Hadid's fuzzy belly. He entered her easily. Love was the occupation of the unoccupied, and aside from working on the occupied building, they had no work.

"Nothing's as real as this embrace," Hadid whispered in her ear.

He was fond of making references to reality and concreteness but they were rarely so tied to daily existence that, more often than not, he lost his listeners with abstract rhetoric. Adina knew the genital embrace corresponded with Hadid's idea of autonomous activity superseding work. At first she found it difficult to occupy her time with games of love that openly ridiculed labor and whose only end was bringing more pleasure to existence. She had grown accustomed to demeaning work by performing ablutions for rich women on a strict schedule. Now time took on a more musical quality akin to the cycles of fingers on her clit or the beat of a belly on her bottom, marking time with an obscene autonome clock.

Hadid took his time. He would inevitably occupy most if not all of her orifice, but he wanted to draw out their intercourse as if he were now making the first remarks in a long conversation. From behind, his cock glided back out, then across her vulva, keeping constant pressure on her moist tissue with its rigidity alone. Most other women would have been able to look down and see the bulbous tip of Hadid's member as it overshot its target. Adina's view was obscured by her large breasts that begged for attention. Hadid's hands were either occupied or in no position to do her any good. He was well aware that if one touched Adina's hot nest, her breasts became jealous.

"Suck them," Hadid murmured.

Adina needed no encouragement. With her right hand, she lifted her nipple to her lips and licked the pink tissue using broad, slow strokes. No one, not even Hadid, knew how to suck a breast as well as Adina, but both nipples at once was a bit of a bother—she pushed them up with two hands, strained her neck and stuck out her tongue as far as it would go. She could lick but not suck both nipples at once, which is what she liked.

She needed the other for her complete satisfaction, and the same was true with her nether regions; there was nothing both so satisfying and empty as onanism. During the course of masturbation, Adina would summon vast armies of studs to service her every whim. These were illusions created by her imagination and, in effect, she turned herself into the other in the world of signs. She loved herself during these moments, but not as herself.

She could touch herself perfectly, experience orgasm instantly. Yet she always realized that the desire she had for herself was the desire of an imaginary other for her. Every taboo she broke in her autoerotic dreams respected that taboo, leaving intact the line between her imaginary transgressions and physical reality.

In contrast to the egoism of onanism, the desire of an actual other—say, Hadid—allowed her to love herself for being loved. She could see herself through Turkish eyes, as the one who was loved. This glimpse of herself in the other helped her transcend ego and realize love for the other. She didn't simply love his love for her. She loved him for loving her.

Nothing is as good as a this, Adina thought to herself as Hadid burst into her and she sluiced down on his cock. She involuntarily eased her leg out a bit, as if trying to hold him inside her to prevent his escape. Hadid did indeed love Adina as much as he loved the other women of the collective. He had no fear of the incest taboo known as sororization; Adina and the other women were simply his soul sisters, whom he married in bed.

With his powerful hand, Hadid massaged Adina's shoulders, kneading the muscles and tendons down her back, then scratching lightly over her buns. He felt her shiver as he bit her neck and caressed the base of her spine. Her tit fell out of her mouth. Adina pulled away and rolled on her back, still holding her tits.

"Suck these," Adina hissed as she pushed her breasts together. Hadid's mission in life was to exalt women—he was free of the culturally dominant distortion that, as a man, he would dominate women. If Adina wanted her breasts sucked, he happily obliged while mounting her again. Hadid had transcended his gender role and when he played it, he jumped out of his armor and laughed at himself. Amour, not armor, was his watchword, and passion wasn't a prelude to optimal relations with women but the end in itself.

Hadid replaced her hands with his, cupping the sides of her breasts. Determined fingers pulled her nipples into his mouth. He flicked tonguestrokes along the sides, swirled over each nippletip. Her breasts bridled against his hands, begging for gentle squeezes. He responded, rounding out her breasts as she entered a sublime state. She worked her hand between their bodies to her clit and instantly fell into the abyss. A low groan issued from her trembling lips, but she didn't quite come.

Hadid ran his tongue down her belly, pulling out of her pussy as he did so, moving with quick kisses to the place where his cock had been. He licked Adina, loving the taste of her lightly fragrant juices. She did finally come in his mouth, but he kept at it, gently and lovingly licking her postorgasmic pussy back into fucking shape. Levering his cock back inside, reeling from the heady scent, he loved her with a long powerful stroke. She raised her legs over his shoulders, and Hadid felt his power grow inside his lovely young sister. This sensation of strength made him weak—he was moved by weakness to the verge of coming. He pulled out and slapped his cock with the back of his hand to stave off ejaculation. The sight of her lovely breasts pressed against her thighs, bulging with taut curves, kept him on the verge as he sank back in. He traced the outline of her left side as her legs descended and twined with his. She wreathed around him and writhed beneath him. With each surge, she sucked in her breath.

He gritted his teeth, and to waylay orgasm, grabbed her around the waist and rolled her on top. His stomach muscles strained as he raised himself, sitting up to suck her breasts, first one, then the other. The tension overwhelmed him. He lay back, the full length of his *leidenschaft*, his passion, inside her. Pushing on Hadid's thighs, she raised herself by her arms and lurched forward, her breasts swinging wildly as she rolled and groaned.

Hadid's world dimmed and heat rose in his head. He held her under her breasts and lifted her off him. Before she could protest, Hadid scrambled behind her, spread open her hair-lined lips and mounted her again with a fury of movements that buckled her body at the waist. She held herself up by her elbows and pushed back at Hadid. Her slightly bulging ass felt elastic under him; it excited him to distraction as he raged in and out. His fingers slid along her neck and wound in her silky hair—he grabbed a fistful and growled under his breath. She felt the heavy swing and bounce of his balls against her inner thighs. With a massive thrust, he forced her flat on the carpet floor—snatched her hand with his free hand and guided it to her clit. Wisps of curly wet hair merged with their tissue-delving fingers.

Adina loved being loved from behind while loving herself. Hadid's hands fell back from her head and pussy; they grasped her buns tightly. He felt her pussy constrict as he rode like a bull gone mad with desire, almost oblivious, for a mad instant, of Adina.

His senses partially returned and he held himself up with his arms—sweat dripped on her back, running into the dimples above her buttocks. He fucked her with insane gyrations that disturbed her masturbation. She paused and moistened her fingers with her tongue, and as she did, she threw him a glance. With a sigh, Hadid loved her more gently, lest her fuse fizzle out. Hadid's blood flowed from his slowly probing member to his arms—he watched the blood distend the veins in his forearms and biceps; he again tightened his grip on her ass.

No, not yet, Hadid said to himself. He pulled out, rolled her over, onto her back, and straddled her torso, his staff coursing between her jutting breasts then parting her lips and gliding into her mouth. Adina's cheek swelled from the inside out—she shot him another glance as she sucked. She was an excellent cocksucker and knew it, caressing the shaft with her hands as she licked and kissed the head, hefting the hairy scrotum in her tiny hands. Hadid nonetheless pulled away from this port and sailed back at full mast through the channel formed by her breasts, then navigated to the ocean of secretions between Adina's legs.

Adina began to curl inside the envelope of orgasm as Hadid held himself by his arms again and sucked her nipple that turned slightly outward. She wanted him to slow down but there was no stopping him as he flowed into her. Adina shuddered again, letting out a quivering groan while tearing through the envelope.

"Ich komme[28]," she said in a strained voice.

Adina loved to be surprised. It was only when she was taken (the 'prise' of surprise meaning just that in French—capture, taking, prize) by Hadid that she attained the most potent satisfaction, still inhaling sharply through spasms and gushes. As for Hadid, it was the powerful orgasm he engendered that triggered his release. Her head clouded over and sleep carried her away. He slipped out and painted her ass with white splotches—white on white in a way that reminded him of the electricity and the latent power in her sleeping pussy.

---

[28]  I'm coming.

# CHAPTER 18

Click. Albert woke with a revolver at his temple. He'd only begun to doze off in the torpid light of dawn, a time when seconds stretch and fade like music. His head still spun with sultry fragrances from Jutte's pussy. She was stretched out next to him, on the other side of the bed, extending her arm with the gun in hand. Red dawn in Berlin as weak rays streamed through the leaden sky, filtered as they were through low clouds. He looked sideways at her with bloodshot eyes.

Her wild-eyed look triggered thoughts in Albert about filming her vagina as the true vent-hole to her soul. The mattress undulated and she groaned with her jerky breaths while clambering to her knees. He wished she would be still because when she moved the gun dug into his temple. She threw him a downward glance, he blinked from a bit of sweat that oozed into his eyes. Her lightly bruised breasts jiggled as she spoke.

"You think guns are sexy?" Jutte dug the barrel into his skin. "Don't you?"

"I think you're sexy." He inhaled deeply and a feeling of death filled his lungs. "Don't misunderstand me, I say it as a compliment."

She'd acquired the revolver during the last fascho attack; Albert had been wrong to assume that the high priestess of freedom was too naive for a power play. No, Jutte was the oldest daughter who had read her Alfred Adler and half-remembered some of what he said about feelings of inferiority. She ran the gun across Albert's forehead to his right temple and faced him, stuffing her breast in his mouth.

"Are my tits sexy?"

He nodded.

"Why don't you make a little video of me and my gun? We could make a bundle of money. You'd cut me in, wouldn't you?"

Jutte again dug the barrel into his skin. Albert moaned into her breast and stiffened against his will.

She pulled herself out of his mouth. "You'd want to exploit my body, wouldn't you?"

"I admire your body and I bet a lot of other men would too."

"Your attitude toward women makes me sick."

"Tell me you don't like to be admired," Albert gasped.

As much as Jutte hated the spectacle, she actually wanted to be objectified, to be the object of desire and then see herself through the distortions of the lens, ideally an anamorphic lens that would make her thinner. She leaned back in bed with visions of the Weimar debauchery and depravity in her head, but kept the gun pointed at Albert.

"I'd be betraying my sex," she said.

"If you don't do it—" Albert glanced at his camera equipment strewn across the hardwood floor. "You'd betray your sensuality."

Jutte lowered the gun, stalked the near empty room. She tried to dissimulate her desire by creating a false dilemma, but in doing so she underscored her desire to star in a repertoire. A real dilemma. Albert reached for the camera, picked it up and pointed it at the black pistol on her white thigh.

"You objectify women with pornography," she said, her tone desperate as she imagined moving her act from the studio to hotel lobbies and nightclubs to shatter the distinction between the spectacle and everyday life.

"Jutte, my dear, you're the subject. The camera is the object and I'm merely an innocent bystander. Think in terms of you and the camera."

Jutte opened the revolver's cylinder and looked through the chambers as the industrial percussion of Einsturzende Neubauten filtered through the walls from the room next door. The camera's eye—quickly refocused by Albert—witnessed that all but one chamber were empty. She snapped the cylinder shut with the flick of her wrist and spun it with her fingertips.

She stormed to the window and looked out, her white, breast-jiggling body bathed in the orange morning light. Albert crept toward her. She turned and started in his direction. He stopped—backed up, still shooting video, until he felt the door. Fumbling for the knob with one hand while focusing on the revolver pointed directly at the lens. The antique knob caught the freshly painted latch. Jutte moved to point blank range, held the gun with two hands, her breasts pinched together. The sun rose a notch. Elsewhere in the building, a woman cried in ecstasy.

"Innocent bystander," Jutte said sarcastically as she pulled the trigger and a shot rang out.

The bullet pierced the lens and Albert's eye. He couldn't speak and only barely saw through one eye in the last gasp of his lungs. Death instantly filled the room. Over and over, she pulled the trigger in knee-jerk rage as force devoured life before a deathless sun.

"Cameras, men," she grumbled while looking down on Albert crumpled on the floor in front of the door as blood flowed from his eyes and other holes in his face.

Adina and Hadid heard the shots.

"What was that?"

Hadid listened for another shot. "Shhh."

They lay still in silence and then heard a siren. Adina moved to the window.

"What is it?" Hadid asked, coming up behind her.

"An ambulance," she said, gazing off in a daze while listening to the sound as he stroked her head. "It's too soon to be related to the shots. The question is, who is doing the shooting?"

"And who go shot, only I'm afraid to ask," he said.

"Do you hear—that sounds like police sirens approaching," she said.

"The GSG-9[29] is probably not far behind," he said. "I need to get out of here."

Eluding others, Jutte found her way to Adina's room and cracked the door—she moved in with her eyes glued on Hadid.

"What happened?" Adina asked.

Jutte turned to her. "I shot this indie film guy."

"Shit," Hadid said as he hurriedly dressed.

The lovers ushered Jutte out the back. They piled in Adina's Trabant, newly bought but quite used, which was now adorned

---

[29]   Grenzschutzgruppe 9, the counterterrorism unit of Germany's Federal Police.

with paintings of falling bombs. Jutte drove, glancing at Hadid in the backseat from time to time and following Adina's directions, retracing in reverse the route she, her mother and grandmother took to the wall when it opened on the west. Stay focused on the here and now, Adina thought as they raced into outstretched sunbeams.

A plane took off from Tempelhof Airport in the center of Berlin. Now that they no longer suffered from wall disease, Adina ceased to wonder where planes were going. What's important is where I'm going, she thought. As they drove along one of the city's big boulevards, Hadid reached over the front passenger seat and handed Jutte a bottle of wine. She took a long pull while holding the wheel with one hand.

Adina glanced at the massive, soot-blackened facades of a Nazi building that had been used by the socialist state and thought about her training at cosmetic school: anatomy, hygiene, nutritional science, etc. When the east was red, she had gone in a short time from her dermatologic residence to being manager of a beauty salon—as though the move was as short as a fashion runway, where she'd also worked part time. She again regretted for an instant not having slept with the manager of the modeling agency.

When the wall came down, the salon work was different. Instead of promoting what she understood as sound customer relations, which she clearly practiced with Albert, in the strictest sense, she was now charged with the sale of products and treatments—above all else. Now that she lived in the squat where laws were made by oneself, she began to see it was for good reason that "no one is in control" was written on wall after wall in their part of town. They were not controlled by someone but by an intricate web of social relations.

As they proceeded through suburbs into the countryside, Adina felt a deep urge, from where she didn't know, to be defiled by Hadid's barbaric lust. The road jutted out on a lakeside peninsula—the serene blue surface drew Hadid's gaze, then turned red and yellow from leaves in glassy water. Jutte hugged the curve through a high-speed turn.

"Slow down," Adina said to Jutte. "Turn here."

Jutte turned.

"Just a little ways farther," Adina said.

Jutte spotted someone who looked like Richard working in a chain gang, cutting the field next to Adina's home with a scythe.

"I'm sorry," Jutte said, "but I can't believe this."

Adina grabbed the bottle from her and took a drink. They passed the spectacle of a large man slicing brush. Adina's father guarded him with a gun and didn't recognize the car because of the bombs painted on it.

"They'll be gone soon," Adina said. "My mother will have them leave."

Jutte shook her head. Adina turned away—it was strange for her to see her father, through the windshield, side-by-side with prisoners who looked like former policemen or even Stasi agents. The chain gang was there on orders from her mother, the village mayor, Adina was sure. She looked back, not believing her eyes, to see her father training a rifle on the biggest ex-Stasi turned unterwelt bruiser, Richard.

"Drive up a bit and pull over," Adina said.

They went on a ways, and Jutte edged off the road and shut off the car. They got out. With her half-shave Berlin bob, her @ tattoo, scruffy shoes and clothes, Adina went unrecognized for a moment. As she, Jutte and Hadid emerged from the car, only Peter barked and ran to greet Adina.

"This is private property," her mother began as Adina and Hadid approached. "You young people can't just go where you please."

"I was born here, remember?"

Adina bent to pet Peter, half-remembering her old dolls, bed and glass-bead jewelry. Her mother's eyes flashed from her daughter and dog to Hadid.

"Adina?"

"Listen, Mother, you don't really own this land any more than you own the air or water. We're going for a swim, and there's nothing you can do to stop us, right Hadid?"

"Günter!" Beata yelled.

"I'm working, woman—can't you see?"

A black fly buzzed by Hadid's nose. He remained silently amazed at the way Adina so naturally internalized the autonomes' right to the world. His mind danced from Proudhon's ability to find theft in property to the genesis of ownership, according to Vico, in capturing slaves during a military occupation—not in the civilized way Romans acquired ownership in private transactions. The fly zipped away as sheared grass blew up in the air. Adina glimpsed sickles glittering in the rising sun but didn't dare look back at Richard and her father.

As she neared the water, Adina felt for her jean buttons. The crusty material collapsed on itself when she pushed it over her round humps. Her tee shirt flew off and the chain gang marveled at her, seen from behind, breasts extending beyond her back with every pendulous wiggle. She tiptoed into the chilly water. A veritable nymph in the pond, Hadid thought. Peter raced into the water ahead of her. Hadid hadn't much noticed the vaguely Herculean figures working by the road, preoccupied as he was by the aura of organic sensations emanating from Adina's ass. He kicked off his boots, trying to identify the source of her sensations—the lake, her dog, defiance of her mother—then stepped out of his trousers and into the water.

Adina twirled on her toes and splashed her Peter. At the first splash, the men completely stopped working. They followed Günter behind the house and watched Adina abandon the dog and nestle in at the water's edge, disclosing the tender pink hole lined with matted fur. "She has mud in her cunt," one of the workers said loudly as Hadid slid next to her. Their laughter was lost with her as her the flesh of her breast shivered at his warm touch, which moved along her legs and hips. He dabbed water into her thin cunt lips and the soft, crinkly hair that softened with more moisture.

"Hadid," she said while breathing in deeply.

He turned to her and traced the swooping curve at the base of her spine that jutted into full, round buttocks, swelling flesh that bulged beyond his grip. She rocked her hips and raised herself. He spanked her.

"You can spank me harder," she said.

His hand switched her white tail. The crack rang out for her father and the chain gang to hear, and as he removed his hand they all saw red marks. He slapped her again and she moaned and curled her lips at the sound, the stinging sensation. The sound died in her open mouth.

If strongholds marked frontiers dividing what was theirs from foreigners, the so-called sacred altars for Romans, Hadid thought, then Adina broke free by smashing sacred images of herself and crossing the border into a realm where sensuousness expanded beyond skin color. Free of the jurisdiction of her parents, free from Richard's strong hold on her, she shattered their boundaries, which were once tightly drawn around her. Hadid liked to think she was finding asylum with him, the foreigner who occupied her sacred altar. Her father, who seethed with rage, was momentarily in need of an asylum of a different sort. He rushed down the slope to the water's edge, stopped and raised his gun. Without an instant of hesitation he shot the Turk in the back with buckshot. His daughter's radiant skin was instantly stained with Hadid's blood.

# CODA

If Albert had rigged a hidden camera in Jan's suitcase—the suitcase the Polish clerk longed to use to go to Saint Petersburg or Paris—the cameraman could have broken into the writer's inner sanctum by remote, still honoring the DO NOT DISTURB sign taken from the State Hotel that was hanging on the doorknob. Had Albert done this and focused on Jan instead of Jutte, he would have seen a man sweating at his writing desk: bloodshot eyes, red nose, yellow teeth—his head in his hands at the onset of a headache after having concentrated creatively for too long at a stretch.

Jan pulled his slightly wet shirt over his head. As he jerked his shirt back, the button scratched his forehead. Oblivious, Jan shuffled a cig out of its pack. Shreds of tobacco scattered on the desk. He struck a safety match, it went out. Sweat dripped on his manuscript as he leaned over the desk, lighting the cig by the emergency candle, watching the game that fire played with itself in his Brecht glasses.

Unlike Anne, Jan put no store in dreams. Consciousness, attained after hours at the writing desk, was what counted to him. The manuscript pages glowed in the flickering candlelight. "What sensuousness recognizes as real, art can represent as actual," Jan wrote with blue ink in an open letter to his censors, "while still veiling some of what is hidden, so long as it doesn't aspire to be art but what is here and now."

Life and art, art and life—like an ass chasing its tail or twisted grass in the bottle, dried from the furnace next door and its excessive heat. To understand love, he thought with this metaphor for his artistic hedonism in mind, one must study all aspects of life. The thought alone was exhausting and Jan fell back in his straw bed while smoking and gazing at the matrix of pipes that hung from the patchwork ceiling: cast iron, copper, galvanized pipes suspended by steel tape; rods and clamps attached to sheets of asbestos, tin and the original wire mesh and plaster riddled with holes.

"How quickly they've learned to love their water," Jan said out loud to himself as he heard a toilet flush and the tainted wave roll down the cast iron pipe near the ceiling. "All is water," he uttered after Thales, feeling the first drops. The sensation didn't startle him, although it should have. He was losing consciousness after spending many intoxicated hours lost in representation. He didn't trust his weary eyes. The waste pipe buckled near a seam—the sound of a distant siren approaching. A man yelled elsewhere in the building.

The cast iron pipe suddenly snapped from the weight of waste now spilling into the room. What the hell, he thought. The broken ends fell on copper pipes that supported the weight for an instant but quickly began to bend. A vent duct broke, knocking over the candle, which set his manuscript on fire. If there weren't cops outside, he would have yelled—he yelled anyway. Nobody came.

A swastikalike twist of scalding pipes crushed Jan into the bed of straw. He felt a rib crack. I'll drown in shit, he thought, remembering how the sewage workers of Warsaw had the balls to be the first strikers. The wall's thick bricks loosened. Shit filled the room, encircling his body as a rotten board went up in the flames from his manuscript. "Time to learn how to die," he said to himself out loud. The ceiling quaked and gave way. Branded and suffocating in a hail of shit. Buried alive in a Berlin ghetto without getting to Paris or Saint Petersburg, without finding his *ultraphilosophe* or Mashinka, without giving existence to his thoughts . . .

# COLOPHON

Originally published as Stasi Slut by Masquerade Books (1991), this novel was subsequently reprinted in small runs as The East Is Black. The first Backbone Books edition (1994) was spiral bound, abridged and numbered less than fifty; the second (1995) was bound by hand in an unnumbered edition estimated to be under 200 copies. The SexPol Editions version (2001), which is listed as the "third edition," was printed in one run of 300 hundred copies and another of 100. Changes were made in a 2006 edition, and following the drafting of a screenplay based on the novel in 2014, the author made the latest revisions comprising the fifth edition (2015).

Printed in the United States
By Bookmasters